THE TOR

POWER SPOTS FORESHADOWING TIME TRAVEL

LIZ K. O'NEILL

CONTENTS

Chapter 1   Huh? 1

Chapter 2   The Foreshadowing 5

Chapter 3   Ground Hog Day Reinvented 9

Chapter 4   The Shed 13

Chapter 5   Swirling Emotions 17

Chapter 6   Time 21

Chapter 7   Comparing Notes 25

Chapter 8   Heebie Jeebies 29

Chapter 9   Woosh 33

Chapter 10   Mussels and Mushrooms 37

Chapter 11   Puddle-Jumping 43

Chapter 12   Burnin' Daylight 47

Chapter 13   Mary and Michael Crossing 51

Chapter 14   The Mix 53

Chapter 15   Why the Stutter? 57

Chapter 16   Karaoke Anyone? 61

Chapter 17   Bam Bam 65

Chapter 18   A Chilling Sight 69

Chapter 19   The Spiritual Gauntlet 73

Chapter 20   Stark Truth 77

Chapter 21   Wearing White 81

Chapter 22   Teeter Totter 85

Chapter 23   Whaat No Coffee? 89

Chapter 24   The Meeting 93

Chapter 25   Penance 97

Chapter 26   More Answers 101

Chapter 27   A Particular Friendship 105

Chapter 28   Not Another Zachary Situation 109

Chapter 29   A Storm is Brewing 113

Chapter 30   Reflecting Positivity................................117

Chapter 31   Concerned Direction 121

Chapter 32   Cacophony Erupts 125

Chapter 33   Deception 129

Chapter 34   The Mask..133

Chapter 35   Ripped Robes 137

Chapter 36   Sheep Without a Shepherd.......................141

Chapter 37   The Knock on the Door 145

Chapter 38   A Familiar Tapping...................................149

Chapter 39   The Shuttle Eaves-Dropping 153

Chapter 40   Processing Begins 157

Chapter 41   The Dishwasher..161

Chapter 42   Revelations..165

Chapter 43   Counting Sheep 169

Chapter 44   The Reckoning 173

Chapter 45   Chapter of Faults 177

Chapter 46   A Surprise to All 181

Chapter 47   Stockholm Syndrome...............................185

Chapter 48   The Staircase..189

Chapter 49   Communication Problems 193

Chapter 50   Visions of People......................................197

Chapter 51   We Know Who You were...........................201

Chapter 52   Slow the Cadence.....................................205

Chapter 53   Healing Takes Place..................................209

Chapter 54   The Summit 213

Chapter 55   The End of the Story.................................217

ACKNOWLEDGMENT

I'd like to acknowledge the two ladies who invited me to England and accompanied me on this trip. It would not have been possible without them. I was inspired to write the time-warp episodes by the one who is named Cordelia in my book. She does past-life readings, so when she said, "We were here," it confirmed for me that I had been in that monastery in the 16th century.

ABOUT THE AUTHOR

LIZ K. O'NEILL, a third-generation Vermonter, has a master's degree in education and a minor in language arts. She spent twenty-eight years living in a religious community. For twenty years, she taught writing and literature to students in grades 6 through 10. She developed curricula for both undergraduate and graduate courses at the local college, where she taught for seven years.

At the same time, she developed an extensive educational website called Imbalance in Relationships while working for approximately 30 years at a women's advocacy shelter. She most recently retired as a Mental Health Worker from a psychiatric/substance abuse treatment program. She has a keen interest in archaeology.She has recently finished writing several books, including *Be Wee With Bea Parts 1 and 2*, a chapter book series, and *Traffic,* a fictional narrative based on extensive research about the rescue of Native American teenagers from a human trafficking operation. The last book on the list, for the time being, is this book, *Tor: It Looms and Leads*. This book is an account of an actual trip the author took to England. It was tweaked to include a fascinating twist—time travel into the16th century.

She is currently working on the third installment of the *Be Wee With Bea* series.

She is also finally nearing the completion of *A Particular Friendship*, a book that she has been working on for over twenty years. This book is about her time at the convent—before, during, and after she left.

NOTE TO THE READER

I'm pleased you've opened up to this page. This is a fascinating book about my trip to England with friends. I started by writing a real-life narrative up to Chapter 18 and portion of Chapter 19. The majority of the story is set in the 16th century. There are 'easter eggs' or as I call them, examples of foreshadowing in Chapter 1 onward, until it becomes clear why the characters had such past-life reactions. See how many you can backtrack on.

INTRODUCTION

Are you familiar with ley lines, which are energy lines that run through the earth's crust? After reading this book, you will know how being in their area can have a drastic impact on your life. If you've never traveled to England, you will feel as if you have.

Follow the journey of our two main characters, Cordelia, a harpist, and Madeline, our narrator, as they weave their way through and around dark energies until they are vortexed into a 16th-century monastery, where they will be beheaded.

PREFACE

I was extremely fortunate to be invited to join in an adventure through the various power spots in England. I was inspired to loosely journal the fascinating and life-changing events we experienced. I wanted to spice up the book by adding the fictitious incident of time travel into a Benedictine monastery in the 16th century. This choice was therapeutic because it resembled the beginnings of my 28 years in a Convent in the twentieth century. The trauma caused by the time travel ordeal and the Tor itself is clarified and resolved at the top of Glastonbury Tor.

CHAPTER 1

············

Huh?

CORDELIA CALLED, yelling so loudly into the phone that I had to turn the volume down. I must have lowered it too low because I missed everything she had said.

Raising the volume, I was able to catch her last few words.

"So, Madeline, can you go? Huh? Please." She pleaded. "You're the only one I'd want to take. Get your Juju going and find all the energy places there, so we can be tourists on my days off or hours off."

Totally confused and not knowing all the details, I was hesitant to commit myself to something I'd regret. She just kept going, so I had no chance to get in even one question, especially the chief one, "What did you say?" Maybe a second question: "What are you talking about?" To heighten the level of mystery, she went on to give information about a place that has yet to be revealed.

"All of us who are going to be taking the harp therapy class have been planning a cool ceremony," she explained. "We want to play our harps in a procession around a giant labyrinth on the Tor; you'll love it," she said, singing the last part an octave higher than her talking voice.

Whatever "the Tor" was, I nodded and said aloud, "Hmmm." Hoping to fill in all the blanks that were being formatted in my mind.

"It'll be quite a hike," she added. "The Tor appears to be formed by the path to a very old labyrinth spiraling around the hill seven times and ending at the top."

I still had no idea what she was talking about. It did sound like a project that would leave us huffing and puffing. How could they play a harp while drudging in circles around a steep hill? I imagined it to be like the Guggenheim Museum in Manhattan, New York City, although the rate of incline didn't strike me as gradual or as user-friendly.

When she took a moment to catch her breath, I knew it might be my only chance to ask those two questions and apologize for not having heard a thing she'd said before the words "So Madeline, can you go, huh? Huh?" came.

She tsked a few times, huffed, and whined. "I don't think I can get as fired up as I was. That moment is gone; that ship has sailed."

When she summarized what she had originally said, it was my turn to break the Richter Scale. "Whaaat? Are you for real? You want me to go with you? Really? Me?"

"Yes, you. As I said, you're my top choice to accompany me," she answered.

"You need to pack your pink and purple umbrella with your heavy harp, because I heard it is always raining there, as I've seen on every show on TV, and when do we leave anyway?"

"Two weeks should give us time to plan our packing, for me to make the flight reservations, and for you to research the energy places."

I strolled over to my bookcase. "Ah, here it is, the travel guidebook. I'll drop it off later."

My dear friend designated me to look up some strong energy spots. I am a dowser who deals with energies in the earth and above. Cordelia is what we call an "inner dowser"; she doesn't need to use a pendulum. She just knows.

I think my mother had that same inner sense. I remember when I was three years old, my grandfather taught me to dowse with a willow Y-branch. I couldn't believe the pull of the stick that I was grasping in the manner directed by my Grampa.

As I attempted to hold it steady, it gradually pointed downwards toward what he said was an underground stream of water leading to a pond. My mother always spoke of wishing to learn more about dowsing. Sadly, she passed before there was a newspaper notice of a new dowsing group being formed.

I announced to her spirit, "Ma, we'll be taking these classes together, and we're finally going to get to learn about dowsing."

My dowsing teacher, Bob, taught us about energy channels called ley lines. These are straight lines of magnetic and luminous energy, traveling through rocks below the surface, crossing locations, and circling the entire earth. They have been found to connect many sites holding churches and monasteries named after derivatives of Mary or Michael.

It is quite telling that these churches were built in areas where pagan sites once stood. Way back then, someone knew how to detect powerful spaces, so the churches were probably built there to purify or Christianize specific spots.

Just as we have energy waves throughout the atmosphere buzzing around our heads, so too do we have them within the earth's makeup. The energy below the surface affects the outcomes above. "As above, so below." Two of these energy lines are named the St. Michael line and the Mary line. The Michael line has a harsh, dark feeling to it. Reaching out around the bodies of water, the Mary line gives a sensation of fluffy energy. The church names coordinate with the line that runs through that area.

When we travel from one ley line region to the next, we can sense a noticeable difference in the dimensions of light they emit, whether bright or dim. If we move from the Mary line to the Michael line, we are apt to perceive changes on several levels: physical, emotional, psychological, and spiritual.

As this story unfurls, you will see how these elements have all dysfunctionally unfolded for us.

....

CHAPTER 2

The Foreshadowing

THE DAY arrived. Shuttling back and forth, we had loaded most of the packs, suitcases, and umbrellas into the car the previous night. There were only the harp and our day packs remaining. The trip to the airport was simple and unusually conflict-free. We quickly checked in using our fancy, high-tech licenses.

It was a new thing in Vermont. They must have wanted us to be able to prove we weren't terrorists. We had to bring papers to prove who we were, along with our social security cards. I saw many people being turned away because they couldn't present fancy papers, such as a light bill from their local electric company.

Remember, in school, when you questioned whether you'd ever need algebra? Well, that was the same rampant doubt that surged about all the fol-de-rol to get our license renewed. Just as we found out when we used algebra in its most primitive form, we discovered there was a function for the fancy license. It could substitute for a lot of complicated paperwork.

We flew right through the check-in process and were soon riding on the conveyor belt to the assigned gate. We found seats and did not have to wait long for our flight to be announced.

We knew it was a long journey to travel "across the pond," but we had no idea the smoothness of how things were going would soon change. The next events that happened could have been a foreshadowing of what was to come.

We were scheduled to have a substantial meal. That was good since we weren't going to have any other meal except the proverbial nuts and coke. About halfway into the flight, the "fasten your seatbelt" lights blink above every seat. This was another red flag, or in this case, a red light.

The pilot came on to announce that the ride would be rough. I'll say. It felt like we were going over bumps on a dirt road. I swear, we went over some ramped jumps you might find on a dirt bike path. Back to the topic of our meal. There was only one burning issue, one complication.

Our steward and stewardesses had to remain in their seats, belted in for safety, for nearly the entirety of the last stretch of the flight. As we were bounced and jounced around, our meals were cooking and cooking and cooking.

You know how a meal gets to the point where you can smell the delectable odor wafting your way? Our meals reached that point, then surpassed it, until we began to smell burning starch. Our frozen baked potatoes were morphing into carbon. I'm sure our chicken was shrinking as it shriveled in the intense heat.

When the "fasten your seatbelt" lights went off, the steward and stewardesses quickly busied themselves cleaning up, only to return to their seats to prepare for our descent. The meager plastic cup of Coke and tiny bag of nuts were going to have to sustain us until we found food the next day.

After exiting the plane and retrieving our belongings, we walked next door to pick up our prearranged rental. We were actually in England; we'd made it. It was really happening.

For some reason, neither Cordelia nor I anticipated what we were going to be challenged with. We just stood there, staring at the steering wheel—not the wheel itself, but where it was located. Ooof. Neither of us had ever driven a vehicle with the steering wheel on the right side, our passenger's side of the car. We would soon realize that that was not the worst discovery.

We were going to have to drive in the opposite lane from what we were accustomed to. What would have been an act of self-preservation on our highways was sheer self-destruction on these roads. To raise the proverbial bar even higher, darkness was chasing us.

It was raining, or drizzling, as we will end up terming it. I do not like driving in the rain. I got terribly lost driving by myself in New York, headed for Brooklyn. My friend Marty said I was in an area where I could have gotten my face ripped off.

I've since realized I was asking them where some foreign street was located, which was clearly not a part of their world. That situation could be compared to a lost tourist asking us where a street is in another town.

Cordelia would be the navigator. Upon leaving the airport, we were faced with too many road choices. It probably wouldn't have mattered which one I turned onto.

Just as I began to feel more confident, Cordelia let out a yelp. "No.... What?... How could that be?"

Once again, I had no idea what was going on. I had to get to the bottom of this, and fast. "What?" I asked. "What's going on?" I felt like I do when I am trying to understand why my cat is yowling. She just sat there mewling, looking back, forward, and then back from where we had just come.

"I just saw a sign saying 15 kilometers to London. We're supposed to be leaving London, not driving toward it," she exclaimed.

I put my head back with a gasp of exasperation, covering my tiny terror. She switched on her little map-reading flashlight as I continued driving in the direction we were going—London airport.

CHAPTER 3

Ground Hog Day Reinvented

CORDELIA MURMURED, more to herself than to me. "I've got it. We were originally on A36 and somehow got onto A34; so, we're up here but we need to be down there."

Raising her volume for my benefit, she said in a short breath, "Okay, so you need to take a sharp right onto A339 right up here." She waited until she was certain I had complied. "Good. Now follow this back until we reach A36 again," she pointed.

This happened so many times that I felt like I was in the movie "Ground Hog Day." Situations like this make me realize why I hate that movie. I was about to cry. As my eyes welled up, I noticed Cordelia was feeling responsible because she was the navigator. We comforted and reassured each other.

I must have finally eliminated all the wrong routes. It was like when I tried to get out of Boston, Massachusetts, along Storrow Drive. I can't tell you how many times I realized the exit in my rearview mirror was the one I needed to take. Around and around, I went, until I finally nabbed it.

As unreal as it seemed, we were headed west, a short distance from Torquay, our temporary destination. From there, we would proceed to the town where Cordelia's harp therapy course would be taking place.

Rain was still pounding our heads as we lugged the last of our luggage and packs into the inn at Torquay, named Inn Torquay. We were way beyond our Eastern Standard bedtime and exhausted after well over an hour of frustration. We forgot about our empty stomachs and went right to sleep. The morning was a more relaxed routine. We had coffee and donuts provided by the inn for breakfast. We casually inspected the map to get to the cottages where we would be staying for the duration. We wanted to avoid any repeat performances of the ordeal from the night before.

The trip to Truro was quite simple. We just headed onto the A30 west, then dipped south on the same route. In no time, we saw signs directing us there. We were so confident that we were able to quickly stop at a little "mom and pop" type store. We bought a few things to cook up for supper and to sustain for a few days.

That was a departure from the previous strangling trip out of London. We never would have dared stop anywhere. I don't even remember seeing anything except confusing route numbers. What route name has three digits and a letter in front of it, anyway?

That is a lot to remember and quickly read and process all at once in the dark, in the rain, in a foreign car, on foreign roads, in a foreign country. A few of the contributing factors to our successful arrival were the timing and weather. It was daylight and no longer raining, for the moment.

Cordelia explained one of the demonstrations I would get to see. She said that everyone will be able to experience how different chords affect them due to the way they play it.

"I know you will be fascinated by observing yourself and others and expressing how they were impacted on the physical, emotional, and spiritual levels," she said. "I loved it when I took part in Part 1 of my harp therapy course. It is actually the basis of our participation in promoting healing in individuals," she added.

She said part one of the course was in the central section of the United States a year or so ago. I can't remember where exactly. She had recently been notified that the second part of the course would be held someplace in England, about which we were soon to learn more.

Our ride up the inclining driveway revealed a panorama of small cottages that appeared to be like something from the old world. I'd seen similar ones on some of my favorite British TV shows. I thought they might be staged there as props to create an ambiance.

It occurred to me at that moment that we, in the United States, live in a very young nation. We had no idea how many layers of history there were in that country, which is currently introducing itself to us. Those gray fieldstone buildings with wooden shingles roofs stood there dispassionately housing tragic historical secrets.

Upon entering, the first thing we noticed was not the lovely, quaint furnishings but the energy. Remember how I told you that both of us are dowsers? That, combined with the fact that we are empaths, like lightning rods, attracts bolts of surging energy. We are both as impressive as a hot ball of wax recording impressions.

Attempting to resist a sense of deep sadness, we reminded each other that it was a time for joy. I told Cordelia that if this sense of darkness persisted, we would attend to its source.

It was time to mix with the other cottages and find out which one was holding the classes.

CHAPTER 4

The Shed

I WAS shown where guests would sit during the harp therapy classes until invited in for any demonstrations. I had brought plenty to read, plus I still had more research to do on the energy places we were planning to visit.

I imagined there would be others joining me. It would be fun comparing notes and discovering where they came from. I would be intermittently journaling and gathering material for a fictional book about our United Kingdom visit to various energy spots.

I was somewhere else in my thoughts when Cordelia sat down beside me. Knowing I sometimes went far away without physically moving, she tapped me on the shoulder to get my attention.

"So, we're free 'til tomorrow at 7 a.m., whatever that is in our time at home for our circadian rhythm."

I hadn't reset watch, so I was even more disoriented. I told Cordelia that I hoped our cottage had a clock that was set to the correct time. Otherwise, I will have to do math to figure out the difference between our time and their time here.

I do know that the time here is five hours ahead of what it is back home in Vermont. "My watch says 11:00 so it must be 3:00 in the afternoon here."

Cordelia paused as if inputting and calculating my information.

Becoming animated, she began speaking. "Let's go look around this place; we've got plenty of time before we eat and our eating schedule is really messed up, anyway. I'm feeling drawn to a certain area; I'm not sure why, but I'm willing to bet we'll find out."

Remember when I told you Cordelia was an inner dowser? I was confident she was onto something. We hadn't thought to ask the others if they'd experienced any sadness in their cottages.

"It will feel good to get away from some of the heaviness. Something went on here, either inside some of these cottages or outside on the surrounding lands," I explained.

Cordelia nodded in agreement the entire time I was talking. She stated that she felt she could breathe better out here. She stopped midway through her stretch and her wide yawn. "Look, there's a little building up on that mound."

She pointed to the slight hill. It was difficult to identify what sort of building was up there. It was the size of a shed. Maybe that's all it was—a place where people kept their tools. But Cordelia was seldom wrong.

There didn't appear to be any steps to get there so I grabbed two walking sticks to help us with the steep challenge, which we gently dropped as we neared the building. My eyes welled up with tears as I sensed a surge of energy.

Hugging herself Cordelia said, " I'm getting chills as I get closer to this building."

I nodded pensively. "Something's going on. My throat is all tightened up."

The perceptive one cautioned me, "Let's approach slowly."

We felt a need to take one wooden step after another with reverence. We didn't know why at that moment, but we would soon discover the source of our despondency.

A part of me didn't want to know what shocking, solemn secrets this building held.

In front of us was a showcase window displaying a variety of random items. There was a pack of cigarettes, some loose and some partially smoked.

Letters that were written in different languages with various scrawling handwriting styles. The most poignant items were the small, folded, faded photographs of family members, friends, or significant others.

We were as puzzled as you may be. As we read the typed card identifying the origin of these items, our emotions grew stronger. I was immediately drained. We held hands to brace each other and held our breaths.

"Cordelia, no wonder we've felt such overwhelming sadness." I said, explaining that my dowsing teacher, Bob, told us he knew one of his past lives had been in England, and I believe this is the place; I'm getting goosebumps now."Yes, there is some connection between him and this strange conglomerate of items," Cordelia agreed immediately. "I can strongly sense it."

"You'll be stunned after I tell you what he said happened; you'll see there were a number of reasons you were led up here, to this very spot. Ooof,"

"So, tell me. I think I might have it figured out. I want to see if I'm right," prompted Cordelia.

"Well, do you want to take a swipe at it? Go ahead. What do you think he said and how is he connected to all of this?" I asked.

"You really want me to say? What if I'm wrong? What if I'm way off? Will you think I'm disrespectful? Will you be offended?"

"Cordelia, you are seldom wrong—never way off; never even very far off—so, now I'm curious. Think of it as a little test. So, come on, what do you think he said?"

Our reverent tone and tearfulness had dissipated. It was just as well. You can only carry such a revelation for so long. It just gets too heavy. The spirit is darkened. I turned toward Cordelia, who was staring into the window of the past.

She took a deep breath, put her head down, and raised it with the answer—the "right on the nose" answer. I was amazed, but not really. In all the world, I don't think I could have guessed what Bob had told our group. But she got it.

I couldn't wait to tell Bob what we'd discovered.

CHAPTER 5

Swirling Emotions

CORDELIA HADN'T realized she'd nailed the answer yet. Hopefully, my next statement will let her know. "It was not a coincidence that you had to come to this country, to this set of cottages, to this miniature museum of mourning."Many people say, "There's no such thing as coincidence," and I believe them.

I told Cordelia that her sensing was correct. Bob, who was also an inner dowser, told us he had a vision that in which he was a young boy in England in one of his past lives. He, along with hundreds of other young boys, stayed in cottages before going off to war. Our dowsing teacher believed that he, like most of the boys in the cottages, never returned.I would be telling her something she already knew, but I needed to say it. "That's what all those items on display are, Cordelia. They are fragments of loved ones whose parents, siblings, cousins, and dear friends waited for word of their survival, safety, and return, or maybe they heard nothing and died wondering what had ever happened to those precious little boys." Bob was held close to someone's heart during WWII, and now we know also during WWI.

Cordelia was silent. I stopped talking and joined her in the place she had been transported. I knew she was also envisioning the goings-on around these cottages.

The emotions that must have been swirling around make me catch my breath, a salty taste forming in the back of my tight throat. The terror those boys must have felt. We recognized the source of the deep sadness we'd experienced upon entering our cottage. We realized we were being called to free some trapped spirits.

"Maybe Bob stayed in our cottage as a young boy," I said. Many of the boys had smoked their last cigarette or written home letters that would never be sent nor received over the years.

Reclaiming our walking sticks, we consciously shuffled down toward the cottages. It was time to cook something for supper. My stomach growled with emptiness when I smelled some form of grilled beef wafting from the rear of one of the cottages, a couple down.

While waiting for the chicken to bake, we planned to discuss our adventures for the coming weekend.

"We only have tomorrow, Friday, for my class, which, by the way, you and the other guests will be observing the part I told you about earlier, and then on Saturday, we can hit a couple of the places you've got planned for us; have you thought about a day-long activity for us yet?" Cordelia inquired.

Just as I was about to elaborate, there was a rapid rap on the door. "I'll get it. Coming." Cordelia raised her voice enough, so they could hear her.

She stood at the door for only a moment. "Okay, I'll be there."

Shutting the door, she turned toward an inquisitive me. "Well, what was that about?" I asked.

"They want to meet to talk about playing our harps around some labyrinth on some Tor. You got me. I have no idea. Hopefully, I can find out more tonight. Mm mm...I think our chicken is done."

As Cordelia lifted the chicken out of the hot oven, I swooped in behind her to get the crispy baked potatoes.

"Well, here goes." Cordelia took a deep breath, shrugged, and commented, "This certainly is an odd-looking chicken."

That was my exact thought. I'm sure she was referring to these English farm birds with long, thin necks. We saw long, skinny legs with the feet still on them in the market… and we bought them. We had reported to each other that it's what we seemed to eat most of the time. I usually have chicken this, and she might have had chicken that.

Whether it was our imagination working overtime or it was a fact, the chicken tasted a bit strange. It's a good thing we were hungry and flavored it up well. Fortunately, the potatoes tasted like our American potatoes.

After we scraped the last of our meal from our plates, we sat down with a cup of coffee. I hope we weren't breaking any cottage mores by having coffee and cake rather than tea and crumpets.

"Oh, look at the time," Cordelia remarked. "I've got to get over to the meeting. We'll talk about our weekend plans when I get back."

I opened my mouth to say something but she was already out the door.

When Cordelia returned, there was a choice of which to discuss: our weekend itinerary or the exciting plans her group of harpists had orchestrated. She seemed a bit conflicted—not with what to discuss but about the tenuousness of the labyrinth walk. No one had even examined the labyrinth or known where it was, if it even still existed, or if it ever existed at all.

She mentioned that as their group continued discussing the history of the labyrinth, someone, who probably was not so keen on circling and at the same time climbing the hill, intimated the whole thing just might be a masterful myth. "So, we don't know now; I guess we'll see as the time gets closer.

Enough of that dredging and tell me what you've got planned for us on Saturday," Cordelia said.

CHAPTER 6

··················

Time

I SUGGESTED to Cordelia that we could check out the famous Stonehenge. "Imagine being so close to those stones that we can touch them and sense the ancient energies and stories; I can't wait."

"If we have more time, where should we go next?" Cordelia was curios.

I proposed we head up to the Stone Circle in Avebury. There's little known about the origins of those stones. "The stones we'll be seeing are over 5000 years old," I added.

"I bet that energy is very strong," she said.

I informed her that there is another interesting spot within walking distance called Silbury Hill. "This place will probably give us goosebumps," I reasoned. "It is a prehistoric mound similar to Egypt's pyramids, older than the Stonehenge, with an enormous water-filled ditch around it."

"I can't wait to see that," said Cordelia.

I went on to tell her that the coolest thing about it is that it looks like the Cydonia formation discovered on Mars called. "I've heard of that," exclaimed ly "Isn't that where they discovered a face too?"

I explained how the whole panorama included a pyramid and a mound. "If we were to do an overlay of the map on Mars, Avebury and Silbury Hill would line up."

"I guess we'll see how generous time is to us," commented Cordelia.

She reminded me that time is elastic and that it can be manipulated. "We'll have to work on it, so we'll have plenty of time."

I paused with a sigh. My therapist told me sighing most often meant "if only," so I guess I was headed there. "I'm hoping we'll be able to walk through a crop circle on the way, so we'll have to keep an eye out for grain crops because that's where I noticed they seemed to appear frequently,""This sounds great." Cordelia said looking at the clock on the wall that I hadn't noticed before. We still have tomorrow to experience, so we should get some good sleep.

"Curiously, what does your watch say, anyway? It's 11 here," she said, making a wide gesture to the clock on the floral-patterned wall.

I did the usual finger counting. "I'd say seven. My watch should read seven."

"Okay, let's see what your watch says," said with expression

I looked at my watch and it read "6:00." "Wait, that can't be right."

"It is, if you count right; count back 5 hours from 11," Cordelia remarked laughing. "I observed you count back from 11 including the number 11; start counting with 10, try it."

I didn't exactly understand why, but I followed her instructions and came up with 6. I counted from 6 using the new method, looked up at the clock, and yup, it's 11 right now.

"Oof, math."

After the flurry of our Saturday itinerary settled down, the heaviness of the spirit returned. But this time, I knew its source. I went to bed, promising the boys' spirits that we would release those who wished for it.

A hand tapped my shoulder. "Rise and shine," Cordelia said, "we've got an exciting day ahead of us, and you're going to be a big part of it."

I am usually sluggish after waking up, but the prospect of learning something entirely new excited me, and the early morning light peeking through the blinds spurred me forward.

We rushed through some coffee and a warm, sweet cinnamon roll for breakfast because we didn't want to be late. We were ushered into a waiting area until they were ready for us. During our enthusiastic chatting, we realized we'd each been provided the same limited amount of information.

When they invited us into the instruction area, our excitement grew. Everyone stood in a circle, leaning on the railing. We had entered the room in the middle of the lesson and I noticed there was one person standing in the center.

I didn't recognize the teacher until I heard a voice from the side. "Welcome guests, we're glad you can join us," she said explaining the theories they'd been working on.

"We'll all see the effects that certain chords have on humans, when sounded, whether emotionally, physically, or spiritually."

The woman in the center was told to make herself comfortable on the carpeted floor by lying face up. This was so we could observe her facial and physical responses as the harp chords were played.

The harpists were signaled to play a specific chord. We were to notice the effect that chord had on us while also keeping an eye on the subject on the floor.

I noticed that I felt quite animated. I felt good. The subject sat up and reported that she had become agitated shortly after the chord was played. Several others in our circle agreed.

When there was an opening, one of the participants spoke up, "I felt elated and happy." The others agreed and I joined them. I was pleased that we were of the same mind or spirit.

As the demonstration continued, it became obvious that people's reactions were consistent with one of two groups. When the one in the center appeared to be relaxing the first group felt relaxed, but the other group felt depressed.

That helped me understand why some songs I listen to make me feel very heavy yet others find them soothing.

Exposure to the chord sounds did have an effect on people.

I began to comprehend the principle of harp therapy. How fascinating. The harpist must play some chords around the patient, observe them, and ask how they were affected. The harpist can play the appropriate chords if they are aware of the patient's needs.

When we were invited to return to our original room, we were so eager to discuss what we had just experienced. One of our group members "shushed" us, warning us that we were a little too loud and that we might interfere with our hostess' ability to focus on her instructions.

A few of us in the larger group reacted differently than the others. We were like a microcosm of the larger group. I was excited to discuss this with Cordelia and see how the different chords affected her.

CHAPTER 7

Comparing Notes

I COULDN'T sit still after that. I had to go outside. And it was a beautiful day for a stroll. I went back to the cottage to leave my book and write a note informing Cordelia that I'd gone for a short walk.

Out of habit, I looked at the watch on my right wrist. It was ten o'clock in the morning in Vermont. Without bothering myself with math, I looked at the green clock on the pale-yellow wallpapered cottage wall: 3 p.m. Classes lasted until 4 p.m. I had an hour to do some research.

I was about to leave, my hand on the knob, when I felt overwhelmed, almost smothered, by sadness. I knew what had to be done. I had to talk with them to get their permission. When Cordelia comes back from her class, we'll be able to finally relieve them and give them peace.

No, wait. It is only fair to have Cordelia here when I do it. She should be coming soon. I decided to walk outside to see if anyone else was out there, to pass some time until Cordelia finished her classes.

A couple of "ladies in waiting" had changed into jeans and t-shirts. I wondered if they'd preplanned their contrasting colors. Caren wore a pink shirt and blue jeans, while Karin wore a blue sleeveless shirt and pink jeans. They were seated in matching colored wooden lawn chairs.

The bright colors were a cheery contrast to the monotonous gray of the overcast English sky. The colors seemed to raise the energy level outside. It took away the reminder of sadness that gnawed away at the foundation of these cottages.

They appeared to be chatting in a casual manner to pass the time. When they noticed my approach, they signaled for me to join them. I walked over to them in my purple striped shirt and army green cargo pants. I chose the forest green chair for fun.

"Have either of you or anyone you know felt a sense heaviness in these cottages?" I asked, taking a deep breath and making a sweeping gesture.

"We thought it was just our imagination." Caren sprang forward, her red hair swishing. "Oh, my goodness!" she gasped. "Yes, we couldn't quite put our finger on it, but there is such a strong atmosphere of, uh, what can I call it?" she paused as she searched for the right word: "defeat." Yes, defeat. "I am relieved to hear both of you talk about this," Karin remarked before we could even turn in her direction. She added, "Cyndy and I were preoccupied with what could possibly be causing the sense of hopelessness that we had difficulty sleeping."

I had no choice but to tell them about the building that Cordelia and I had been drawn to. As I recounted our heart-wrenching discovery, the pain I felt resurfaced, and tears began to well up. At that moment, the only sound that can be heard is from some cute chickadees scavenging for seeds in the carpet of green grass. They looked at each other as I explained how I was a spiritual dowser. "I'm going to check with all of the spirits a little later to avail them of the opportunity to be freed," I said, explaining that I needed to get the spirit's permission first since we can never make choices for others, that it is not our business, and we must always respect others. "I would not attempt to move them toward the light without their permission," I said.

"Please do something for them, if you can, please," pleaded Caren. It was clear that their spirits had deeply affected her.

"Yes, please do something," Karin said, adding that she was afraid that the feelings of defeat would sabotage Cyndy's success.I wasn't sure if I was trying to comfort or warn them, so I spoke in a slow staccato cadence. ". . . so, with your permission, I'll put a shield of protection around you on all levels."

"What do you mean by a shield of protection on all levels?"

Karin didn't even let Caren finish her question because it was, of course, hers as well. "Yuh, on all levels? What are the levels? What is on these levels?"

I did my best to explain.

"We're talking about the levels at which we are either healed or harmed. Of course, the most obvious is physical; the next, which slowly becomes evident, is psychological and emotional, or one's perception of life; the third, however, only some people can relate to.

"It is the invisible. It's similar to how the chords of the harp affect us. We don't know. We don't understand why it works, or even how it works, but it works. This is the spiritual dimension we are delving into. All of it is cloaked in mystery."

"Wow, I'm speechless—which is odd for me because I'm usually a chatterbox," Karin said, her hoop earrings clinking as she shook her head slowly.

"I've never heard of or seen harp therapy, nor can I begin to understand how it works, but I guess if you believe you can do good by this, then go ahead," Caren said, being able to express herself better. "We'll have to go check that little building out," she continued.

"Just be ready to experience strong emotions, as Cordelia and I did," I said as distracting, animated yakking pouring from the cottage where the classes were held interrupted our conversation. We got up from our chairs and moseyed toward our respective harp therapists.

CHAPTER 8

Heebie Jeebies

"HI."

"Hi, ready to go rest and talk a while?" replied Cordelia, as she shifted the hand carrying her harp.

"Definitely. We can put some coffee on and snack on the tea biscuits. I hope we'll be okay having tea biscuits with coffee."

I pulled out two metal cans, one yellow and the other blue, as we entered the cottage. The scoop sank into the coffee grounds, stirring up a wonderful aroma. I told Cordelia as I poured out enough water to make a full pot, "I got information about how the sadness we felt permeates the other cottages."

"I got information about the chicken we bought and attempted to eat. Which do you want us to talk about first?"

The coffee pot began to gurgle in the background.

Cordelia grabbed the yellow tin and, using her strong fingernails, pried off the silver lid, but she lost grip, and it was sent spinning, making a cat-like sound of "waal, waal, waal" until it landed with a thunk. While the musical lid distracted me, Cordelia was already grabbing and gorging herself with one of the tea biscuits.

I guess we didn't have to worry about apologizing to the tea gods for breaking the ritual by having tea biscuits with tea. "Boy, you must be hungry," I said.

"Concentroiting mates me hungwy," Cordelia replied.

Is this why we were told as children not to talk with our mouths full? Since the chicken conversation wasn't going to be as serious as my plans for after supper, I said, "So what did you learn about the strange chicken we purchased and attempted to eat?"

Cordelia announced the coffee was ready, and she poured a fresh, steaming cup for each of us. I've heard research has shown that just smelling the aroma of coffee will change a person's disposition and level of energy. Even though it was from a tea cup, that first sip made me a believer in research.

Deciding to be more formal, Cordelia placed some biscuits on a blue-patterned saucer. As we ate one biscuit after another, the image of a cathedral began to peek out. We had no idea this was a colorful foreshadowing of things to come.

"Back to my question, what did you learn about why that chicken looked so different from any we'd ever seen or eaten?"

I noticed that the coffee had a softening effect on the biscuits, especially when dunked. Cordelia was able to chew more quickly and efficiently, making her more coherent.

"First of all, some of the others laughed when I asked about the chicken. As I described what we observed, they glanced back and forth, nodding their heads. I wasn't sure what that meant," she said.

"Well, what information did you finally get from them?" I asked.

"They said it was probably a chicken called the Malay Chicken, which is the tallest or nearly tallest chicken ever. It was introduced to England around 1830," she reported.

"Oof. So that's why the legs were so skinny and long. I wonder if it tasted different because we've never had it before, but it's been around since 1830—wow."

"Yuh, they said that the taste would be affected by the foods they were fed. I guess there are special recipes with spices for this chicken."

"Maybe we should have looked around in these cupboards and dug up some spices to bury that 1830s taste?"Cordelia glanced at the row of cupboards and nodded, rolling her eyes. "Some said it was very tasty with the right spices, so maybe it could have been more palatable. Oh well, now we know."

We had kind of mindlessly eaten from the plate full of biscuits. Another point of foreshadowing was uncovered. We both stared at the images on the plate, then at each other. "I just had this weird wave of chill come over me."

I was stunned that she'd sense something too. "M. . . me too," I mumbled.

Now that only crumbs remained, there was another building resembling the cathedral but not really. We would discover the identity and function of that building in a startling reveal.

"That plate gives me the heebie-jeebies," I said, suggesting that we go over to the couches so we can discuss what I learned about the sadness here and the little building we discovered.Vibrating her lips and hugging herself, "bwooa haw huh haw," Cordelia's whole being shook.

Remember, I said Cordelia is an inner dowser, so she was unfamiliar with device dowsing, so I needed to educate her. She had told me she was looking forward to learning as much about it as she could. Messages just seem to come to inner dowsers. They just have a way of knowing.I didn't totally trust my inner dowsing. Most of the time, I have to double-check with my dowsing device, a pendulum. A pendulum is anything that swings. Some people think they have to have a special crystal of a specific type or color.

I have gently swung my fanny pack when in the grocery store to determine whether to buy a particular product. I want to state a disclaimer here. I did not dowse about the chicken.

An uneasy Cordelia made her way to the couches as if she couldn't put enough distance between that plate and herself soon enough. She sank into the worn-out navy-blue couch cushions, facing me in the brown plaid overstuffed one.

"So, what's going on?" She asked with a curious, concerned look. "Why did you get so serious all of a sudden?"

CHAPTER 9

....

Woosh

"I WANTED to share with you what I got from the ladies whom I was sitting with while waiting for you guys to get out."

"Great! Go ahead," she urged. "I'm anxious to hear what's going on with the others."

"I saw two of them sitting outside and was curious whether anyone else had felt the same heaviness we did, and they gave specific descriptions for how the energy felt to them.

"One said she and Cyndy, who's in your class, were so preoccupied with what could possibly be causing the sense of hopelessness that they had difficulty getting sleep.

"The other termed it a feeling of defeat. So, I told them about our discovery of that little building and what was in there. I told them that we didn't fully comprehend its implications, but we would work on it."

Cordelia posed a question that was gnawing at me. "I do wonder who placed those artifacts there, why, and how long ago."

"We'll probably never know but I do feel they were placed there for us—you—to be led toward. We'd never have made the connection about Bob having been here."

I told Cordelia that I want to invite their spirits to go toward the light and be free. "Depending on how long they've been here, some may be hesitant," I added.

"Whoa, that's great, how do you do that?"

"First, I have to get their permission; we do not have the right to move energy around without permission," I said. "We may have what we believe to be a good agenda, but we must ask permission."

I removed the chain holding my pendant from around my neck.

"Wow, that is beautiful. What is it? It's got several stones in it."

Handing it to her to point out each element, I said, "This is a yoga goddess with a moonstone for the face and an amethyst for the center."

"Is that important to be able to set the spirits free and are those stones the best ones to use?"

I explained that a pendulum is anything that swings and that that pendant had become a nice convenience since I often wear it.

I told her to watch how the pendulum swung so she would know which answer was a yes or a no. I explained to her that a "Yes" is indicated by the direction we shake our heads for a 'yes'—to and from our body; And a "No" by a movement from left to right and right to left. I also informed her that I would ask the spirits if they wanted to be set free.

Cordelia wiggled her legs. "Cool."

"But we need to be calm and focused," I said as she sat back and braced herself.

"We need to have a shield of protection around us because we may open up channels to unwanted energies, which could bring about confusion and imbalance." I spent a moment getting into a reflective state. Cordelia followed suit.

I spun my pendulum in a clockwise motion—my healing technique. I asked for protection for us as we opened pathways for the spirits of these boys to be set free. I moved on to our current mission.

Slightly moving my pendulum back and forth, I began. "We are aware of your sadness, terror, and all that you've lost," I said, nodding to

Cordelia, "and we want to give you the opportunity to be set free, to go toward the light."

Tears welled up, ready to spill onto my warm smile. "Would you like to move on?"

We both watched my pendulum as it moved away and toward me. "If that means yes, do you want us to proceed?" The pendulum signaled another yes.

I began swinging my pendulum in an expansive clockwise circle as my healing action for them and said, "You said you all wanted to be set free, so go toward the light." As my pendulum continued to swing in the healing direction, I repeated my words. "Go toward the light; you will be happier and at peace."

The size of the spinning circle grew smaller until my pendulum slowed to a stop. There was an intense pause in energy; everything was still. We both had our heads bowed in contemplation.

At that exact moment I felt a powerful 'woosh', Cordelia said, "Did you feel that?"

I looked at her in astonishment, "Yes, you felt it too?"

Cordelia described her experience. "I felt spirit energy zoom from the tips of my toes, up, up, and out through the spiritual opening in my head."

"I felt something move from my gut to top of my head through the center."

I rotated my head as if I were sniffing the environment of the room. "I don't feel that sadness now," I said as I got up to check the feeling in the kitchen and looked upstairs. "Nope, nothing."

Cordelia joined me in the stairway. "So, are they gone?" she asked.

"It feels like they are." With a desire for confirmation, I said, "We'll have to check with the others; hopefully, they'll have noticed a difference."

Cordelia named some people she'd ask.

"Well, you've got to be up bright and early tomorrow for your last class of the week," I said, breaking into song for the next three words. "Then comes Saturday." I twirled around, bowing at the word "Saturday."

CHAPTER 10

Mussels and Mushrooms

IN THE morning, the smell of freshly made coffee wafted up to my room. In contrast to the day before, the air was light and cheery. The sun was shining for a change, casting beautiful shadows through the pale green drapes. I rose to invite the warmth of a new day.

While we, the nonparticipants, were in our familiar busyness room, I took advantage of a perfect opportunity to see if anyone had noticed a difference in the darkness and depression, which they may have sensed before the lost and trapped spirits were set free.

I chose to approach Karin and Caren because they would know why I was asking the question right away.

"Caren and Karin, remember our conversation from yesterday and the descriptions of what you've been feeling throughout your cottages? I was wondering if you noticed anything different when you woke this morning."

Once again, Karin spoke before Caren. "I told Cyndy of our conversation and what you had hoped to do for those boys," she said, adding that they awoke differently this morning. She intended to wake Cyndy up, but she was already singing her heart out in the shower.

"I opened the drapes and let in the bright light; I'm on the east side so I get the best of the sun if it's not dark, dreary and raining, which it does a lot in this country; we're from California, USA, so rain is an unfamiliar event for us," she continued.

Caren was absorbing Karin's every word. "I felt like the thick strands of a giant web had been snipped, snipped, snipped and Mary Jo and I both felt less constricted," stated Caren. "Wow, that's all that was necessary? Those spirits must be so grateful."

"I'm humbled I was able to help them out," I said.

Karin asked, and Caren nodded in mutual interest "So have you done this before, released spirits?"

"I work in an old psych hospital, and the morgue is in the deep basement; when I've had to do a one-to-one safety sitting outside a patient's room, I have, over time, been nudged by many spirits to be released," I explained.

Caren popped in a question, "Wow, weren't you scared?"

Karin agreed. "Yuh, that would be creepy."

I shrugged and told them that I just knew that if family or the higher-ups thought it necessary for them to be there, they must have gone through great mental torment.I explained, "This is how it usually happens: As I sit in the evening quiet, I frequently sense a presence to my right, and when I ask if anyone is there, I often feel a positive answer; I dowse to determine the answer after asking if they want to be set free; if they do, I instruct them to go toward the light, and shortly after that, they leave."

"Do others where you work sense them too?" Caren asked for both of them.

I chuckled. "I was amused when one of the staff members asked if I knew of a spirit on the third floor?"

Karin and Caren, both animated, asked simultaneously, "What did you say?"

I told them that I had quietly laughed and explained what had happened to my friend. My friend's response was to exclaim, "Maybe the spirit isn't still there anymore."

The three of us subdued our laughter so as not to disturb the others, who were engaged in conversation or reading.

It was time for me to double-check our itinerary for the following day, Saturday. The list read: Stonehenge, a crop circle, standing stones in Avebury, and hopefully, to top it all off (pun intended), Silbury Hill. The sudden commotion indicated that the harpists were leaving class early since it was Friday.

As I stood there, Karin and Caren invited me and Cordelia to join them and others for supper. I accepted it for both of us, noting that I needed to finalize it with Cordelia first.

As I approached her with my mouth open to speak, Cordelia said, "I tentatively accepted an invitation from Cyndy for us to go out to eat with some others in our group; Whadda ya think?"

She wondered why I was laughing until I told her I had accepted the same invitation.

She laughed, saying, "Well, I guess we're going then. They said it was just a short walk away. We just walk out of here, down Lemon Street. It's called the Longstore, across from Fairmantle Street."

We were there in no time. We mostly mumbled the names of pubs and streets in order to avoid getting lost; no intelligent sentences were spoken. We had a delightful time mingling with everyone.

The jaunt back was no more intelligible than the sprint there. We were with two other people who appeared to be spotting themselves for the same reason. Nobody wanted to get lost in Truro or anywhere in England.

We bid our walking companions good night and went inside, dropping onto our respective couches.

"Ugh, I'm so full; good thing we had the walk back to help things settle," I said. "Cordelia, good thing you like stuffed wild mushrooms, they were monstrous."

"The mussels tasted like somebody had just run down the hill to the water and fetched them because they were so fresh," Cordelia replied, sounding like she could have been a restaurant reviewer by the way she affected her voice and dialect.

"I'll put our white boxes in the refrigerator; do you want to write your name on yours?"

"Nah, I carved a big C with my fingernail on the top of mine."

"And I'll carve an M on mine." I flashed a big smile.

As I was shutting the door, Cordelia asked, "So, could you remind me of our plans for Saturday?"

"Well, we can't say we were here in England without having visited Stonehenge, and I did some serious research while I was waiting for you in what we've come to call our busyness room—I was looking on the map to see where the Michael Line runs around here and if it goes near Stonehenge."

I took a deep breath and let it out, leaving Cordelia in suspense as to what I was going to say next.

As I mentioned earlier, my dear friend designated me to look up some strong energy spots. I am a dowser who deals with energies in the earth and above.

Among many others, there are two basic ley lines running through the world. Just as we have energy waves throughout the atmosphere, so too do we have them within the earth's makeup. The energy below the surface affects the outcomes above. You may have heard the saying, "As above, so below."

The two ley lines of which I speak are referred to as the St. Michael line and the Mary line. The Michael line has a harsh, dark feeling to it, while the Mary line, skirting around bodies of water, has a fluffy energy sensation.

The Michael line is a rigidly directed line, whereas the Mary line forms more of a weaving pattern across England. These two opposing energies do cross each other in several places.

"I discovered that the Michael ley line begins just a few miles away from us, right here; doesn't that make sense now?"

Cordelia sat forward, her eyes wide open. "I guess it certainly does make a lot of sense—that the Michael line must carry massive, mean energy." Pursing her lips while nodding her head from side to side, she asked, "Okay… tell me where else will we meet ol' Michael?"

"One thing I read in my research is that, at least before the 20th century, many believed the churches were built on power plots that were previous Pagan gathering places; so, it seems like these energies were perceived long before churches were built."

"I'm sure we'll see a lot of churches or cathedrals along the way," Cordelia shuddered. "I don't know why that thought makes me want to scrunch up."

CHAPTER 11

Puddle-Jumping

TIPPING MY head to one side, I nodded, signaling my understanding. After all, she was the inner dowser. "After we leave Stonehenge, also on the Michael line, we'll head up to Avebury to experience the Standing Stones," I said.

"Oh, cool, that sounds like a nice change," replied Cordelia.

"Well…"

"Well, what? What now—doesn't ol' Michael reach way up there as well?""Maybe, more significantly, it's where the Mary line crashes into the Michael line; so, there should be very interesting energy there," I said, adding, "When we travel from one ley line to the area influenced by the other, we will sense a noticeable difference; also, I may have originally told you that Silbury Hill is within walking distance from there; now that excites me, because it is. . . well, actually that whole area. . . has been identified as a similar model on Mars."

"Whoopee, so cool!" exclaimed Cordelia. "Now, you mentioned seeing a crop circle; what's that about—is there a model crop circle somewhere there, like a museum?"

"No, I just know we will find one; it's like inner dowsing backed up with my pendulum," I answered.

I told her that when I asked if we'd see a crop circle before arriving at Avebury, the answer was yes, so we shall see. "You should be driving around that time, so I can search the grain fields," I added.

We got started very early. Even in the breaking of dawn with a shy, skinny shard of light showing through dark clouds, Route 39a was simple to follow. Cordelia, remembering my cautionary tale from when we were planning the logistics back home, packed our umbrellas.

"I believe the Michael line will greet us soon." I had not spoken more than I had to when the surrounding clouds grew heavy and opaque. Cordelia's inner dowsing was going to keep us dry.

A steady downpour accompanied us into the parking lot. Cordelia reached toward the rear seat to joyfully grab our umbrellas. We were to line up behind umbrellas that appeared to be the tips of a giant box of crayons.

As we bought our tickets, we were offered a handheld tape recorder. When I looked over to see if Cordelia took one, someone blocked my vision. I accepted one, thinking it would be similar to those handed out at our Alcatraz tour.

The reassuring voice in my gray cassette recorder guided us through the tour with lifelike auditory scenarios, such as the outbreak in the kitchen where a knife was reported to be missing. Over the riotous racket, the narrator directed us to pay attention to the tracings around the knives so that we could identify which knife was no longer in its place.

The most striking thing was that I could sense the spirits, who appeared to have stayed in the tiny, dark, denigrating place where they endured years of their giant timeout known as the "shu."

I've never had a more spiritually moving experience than when we circled the history-laden stones that were restricted by a rope. The untouched monoliths felt miles away; they were definitely measured to be a little under five hundred feet.

There were no sensing energies, commentaries, or answers about this aloof structure. I had to grip my umbrella with the hammering rain in addition to the useless clamor about totally unrelated matters coming from my recorder.At the same time, I was snapping iconic photos with my point-and-shoot camera— the best takeaway from this tourist tryst. What an ordeal! I wondered if Cordelia had gone through anything similar. I would soon find out. We were nearing our path of entrance on the left and would be pointed to the exit on our right.

After returning the still-chattering recorder, I headed for our rental. "Oof, do you remember what our car looked like?" I was yelling over the staccato tap, tapping of the significant raindrops on my sopping umbrella.

Cordelia rotated her body, umbrella and all. It didn't take her any time to "inner dowse" the location of our car. She raised her arm, pointed in the direction we were to walk, and began puddle-jumping, seeing the futility of yelling anything. I followed suit.

Soon, she had the car door open, unlocking my side. I sat slightly on the edge of the seat, closing, opening, and closing my umbrella to shake off the pooling wetness. Cordelia had already figured out how to turn the heater on. This girl is definitely a keeper.

She gripped the wheel and growled, "Brrrr, I thought the heater would add a warm touch to this totally cold experience; what a disappointment—too commercialized."

There was comfort in that car, though. In addition to being warmed by the heat, a psychic friend was validating my perceptions. "So, was it a bust for you too?" I asked. "It is overly commercialized, so I hope you didn't grab one of those non-productive black wands."

The moment the male voice commenced to drone, Cordelia claimed that she immediately turned off that freckle-less piece of plastic. "It wasn't insulting, just extremely annoying," she added.

I wish I had turned mine off sooner. It might have made me more receptive to the energies; I would have felt honored instead of ornery.

"Oh well, the next event, the crop circle, will make up for this crushing occurrence," I said.

Cordelia was still an unbeliever. "If you say so, then it's probably so," she said, raising both arms.

I told her that I dowsed the question a long time ago—will we see and walk in a real crop circle?—and the answer was yes.

"How can dowsing with a pendulum allow you to predict the future? Sometimes I just know something's going to happen but how can a pendulum tell you something?" Cordelia questioned.

"Well, first of all, I'm not asking the pendulum." I told her that when I ask a question for my higher or spiritual self to receive the proper energies, I phrase my question in the future-past tense, for example, "Will we have seen?" That's the best way I can explain it.It was evident that Cordelia was listening to my every word, attempting to absorb the new concept. She hadn't yet put the gear shift into drive when she said, "We'll follow the yellow car to make certain we merge into the correct lane."After maneuvering through the mental gymnastics of English driving, we were on our way. Though we were both in deep thought, I kept an ever-vigilant eye out for the crop circle that I had called forward before we had deplaned days ago.

I saw an old crop circle up on a hill to my right. The stalks were already beginning to grow back as our favorite haircut does, no longer resembling its original style. With heightened hopes, I knew it wouldn't be long.

·················

CHAPTER 12

Burnin' Daylight

WE DROVE onward. Seeing one undisturbed grain field after another, my enthusiasm began to wilt, just like that worn crop circle we passed by way back.

Nearly speechless, I croaked for Cordelia to slow down, "There, up there, to our left, look!" Hardly able to contain myself, I said, "We've got to find a place to turn or do something.""I'll pull over on the left, right over there; it'll be a bit of a challenge, but we can do it." Cordelia waggled her pointer finger a little ahead of us. She couldn't get through the tractor path opening in the fence soon enough.

There in front of us were nine consecutive circles, their circumference increasing as they climbed the hill. I took out my camera and noticed that the insipid rain had ceased and the energy felt different.

"Do you suppose this is the Mary line we're in?" Cordelia asked as she danced around, her words jiggling as she spoke. "I feel that fluffy energy you've mentioned."

"Yes, I think we've left the Michael line behind, for a while anyway; it does feel so good, doesn't it?""At the Stonehenge, it felt like a painful deep muscle massage, and this area feels like a warmed rock massage; ooh, yum."

"You've stated it perfectly, Cordelia," I said.

As we progressed from one circle to another, we stood, arms outstretched wide, to take in the invigorating energy. This was clearly not some hoax fabricated by nocturnal individuals in a grain field creating art. This was the real thing. I thanked whomever it was for bringing one of my dreams to fruition.

There were only a few people around, which accentuated the amiable environment. One smiled and said, "Pretty fantastic, isn't it?" She continued, "Good luck taking pictures, my daughter's camera jammed; I guess she wasn't supposed to have pictures of these."

I swallowed hard as I aimed my lens at the strangely bent, unbroken, thin barley stalks. I couldn't imagine what I'd do if my camera froze at a sacred moment like this.

"Click, click, click." Success. I expelled so much tension that I hoped it wouldn't mix toxically with the surrounding energies. I was so consumed with exhilaration that Cordelia had to tap me on the shoulder to get my attention.

She was having someone take our picture. "Hand this lovely lady your camera so she can take our picture," she requested. With gallant smiles, we corkscrewed our hands and arms once more, receiving the adrenalizing crop circle energy and photographing the moment.As John Wayne said in one of his movies, "We were burnin' daylight," we still had two more stops.

Leaving, I felt heavy-hearted. Cordelia claimed to be feeling dismal. As I put my right foot inside the car, bending toward the seat, I saw it by my shoe. It was a piece of the crop circle.

That, together with the fossilized trilobite stone I found in the ninth circle at the top of the hill, would allow me to bring the energy of the crop circle home. I dowsed to ask permission to pocket the stone and bag the piece of barley.

I wanted something to be able to keep real—one of my most incredible memories. We had no idea that there would be things in the future that we would fight to forget for the rest of our lives.

My pendulum indicated "yes" just before we backed out onto the A361 highway, headed for Avebury. Our hearts and spirits were full. We were quiet for much of the remainder of our trip until we reached signs telling us we were nearing Avebury.

CHAPTER 13

....

Mary and Michael Crossing

SOME SORT of distant pyramid-shaped hill with the top hacked off caught my attention on the left, but to the right were rows and circles of standing stones. There was no one around to take money, tear tickets, or, best of all, dole out worthless tape recorders. This was also where the Mary line influenced the Michael line, or vice versa. We would see.

The light and airy sensation remained. What pressing force from ol' Michael did Mary have to work to neutralize on these grounds?

It hadn't occurred to me until just then that we would not need umbrellas. We didn't use them at the crop circle either. Maybe it was just a little gift from Mary combined with her soft, positive energy.

In my jubilance, I forgot to close my door. Cordelia, familiar with my ADD behaviors, shut and locked the doors and caught up with me. We had discussed our planned approach: to stand at each stone and read the energy.

At the outset, we discerned the energy of those stones to be female. We wondered if each would have her own story. As we stood with the first one, we smiled, sensing a contented, warm joy.

Cordelia expressed my sentiments with a gesture accompanied by a soft, nearly inaudible whisper. I read her lips and her hand motions to mean "Wait, not yet; let's stay right here." I could hear and feel her serene sigh. We just wanted to bask in the secure feeling, one that we had not felt in a very long time.

It was good we had that shot of resilience. I felt as if I'd been struck right in the gut as I neared the next stone. I witnessed Cordelia grab her ribs. This stone was holding great pain for the multitudes. I was picturing throngs of women running for their lives.

"What could possibly have happened to the bearers of this torment?" Cordelia continued with her vision. "At least fifty women were hiding, filled with terror for fear of being captured and restrained."

"Phew, powerful," I said. I wondered where the next one would transport us.

Cordelia chuckled. I looked at her quizzically. "Funny you should mention being transported because this clearly has the energy of a vortex." She waggled her hands from the middle of the stone upward.

I had a strange sense of panic, as if I was going to be transported somewhere else, to another space, in another lifetime.

CHAPTER 14

·················

The Mix

WE AWOKE well-rested. I think the activities from the previous day had tuckered us out so much that it overtook the high level of adrenaline we put to bed for the night.   We placed our sweet rolls on paper towels while we sat with cups of coffee. A few moments later, Cordelia went to get her lovely purple wallet inside her maroon leather pocketbook. She took out an American quarter from the coin compartment, wishing that it had taken her longer to find one since we'd decided to flip a coin to decide who would wash the creepy plate we'd used to serve our biscuits on the other day. I wasn't sure if I could touch the shiny images of the church or cathedral and whatever the other building was if I lost the toss, but the die was cast, and we'd soon know who'd get to wash that dish.

"Heads or tails?" Cordelia asked. I slowly drifted away. —h She asked again.

Oh, great! Now I get to choose my own fate. "Heads," I replied.

She held the ominous coin between her forefinger and thumbnail. I was so focused on how I was going to summon enough strength to overcome my new phobia that I missed the head flipping over the tail, over the head, and landing on her palm.

I obviously went somewhere else because Cordelia had to tap me on the shoulder to get my attention. "Well, guess what it came up for."

A salty taste gathered in my mouth, and my throat tightened. From the tone of her voice, I could not figure out anything, no matter how hard I tried. Her presentation was purposefully flat. "I don't know; I give up." We were in an uncomfortable guessing game, but I was ready. Sue from Life Below Zero was my role model because she gritted her teeth and managed to complete unpleasant and difficult tasks.

But Cordelia surprised me yet again. She headed toward the kitchen sink and said, "Well, I'd better put a shield of protection around myself and get that plate washed." More chills. She made horse-like whinnying the entire time she was touching that plate.

When she returned to the sitting room, she sang in a high-pitched tone, "Please brush my aura, please." Comb the aura is another term for this same request I used to perform on staff members whom I used to work with at the psych hospital. I "raked" the energy from her head all the way to her feet, shaking any negative energy off my fingers, then started at the top again, on another side, repeating the motion until all sides were combed or brushed. She was giddy. "Oh, that feels delicious; thank you, thank you."

That was the end of that. No words were spoken about that dish, its images, or the effects it had on us. We also didn't need to use any of those plates. We managed fine without them. As of yet, we did not know why certain words, thoughts, or images affected us, but we knew it wasn't good and that the day of reckoning was nearing.

Soon after, I arrived at a gathering of new friends, who like me, were learning how to use their harps not just for entertainment, but also for healing. Many were local—from England. Like most of us, they admitted that they had not visited areas that were sought after by tourists.

This is a strange fact. I would never have ridden a gondola or a chair lift in our skiing locations if it hadn't been for the purpose of showing or bringing our friends to a fun place at our local attractions.

This was probably true for this group since they haven't been to Stonehenge, the Standing Stones, or Silbury Hill. However, many of them had seen strange lights in the sky and some had seen crop circles.

"I saw them making your crop circle, late last evening," Caren said in the middle of the discussion, and everyone stared at her, eyes begging for more details. "I saw their lights in the sky just north of here," she added.

One fellow, with whom I was unfamiliar, challenged Cordelia by asking, "So were you sitting out here with a compass? How did you know it was north of here?"

I loved her response. "The big dipper was out, and I spotted it with the North star," she said matte-of-factly, without any trace of smugness. That ended his questions.

Karin mentioned that she'd read there is a great deal of UFO activity near Stonehenge and Avebury, where the Standing Stones are. She said that these are often coordinated with crop circle appearances.It was time for the "devil's advocate" to speak up. "So, how do we know some humans didn't make your nine circles in that grain field? You have no real proof, while some guys proved they made them," I said.

"Oh, like they are hopping on a private jet with their little flat boards and rope and making them all over the world—did you know they are sighted all over the world?" a believer chimed in, "And they are becoming so complicated that it is something scientists have to use a computer for to figure out the equations they indicate."

"Well, maybe there's a club of them," I said. When he wouldn't let up, I knew it was time to change the topic—to drip a drop of nitroglycerin into the mix.

CHAPTER 15

....

Why the Stutter?

"ON ANOTHER subject, are any of you making plans to go with your harpist friend to the G-Glastonbury T-Tor?" I had suddenly developed a stutter. What was that about?"

There were nearly as many different reactions as there were people present. If all nine of us participated, there could be quite a debate. I watched the facial expressions and body movements to spot any reactions similar to Cordelia's and mine. Right off, I noticed five people fidgeting in their chairs.

They would be my intended targets, and it's no surprise that two of them were Karin and Caren. When I first met them, I sensed a connection. I had an odd reaction as we sat calmly reflecting on this whole experience when Caren said, "I feel like we are in a monastery here; it is so peaceful."

Immediately, I became agitated and anxious. I tried to calm down, but kept hearing her say "monastery… monastery… monastery." Here we were facing each other, confronted with questions about things unknown but somehow imminent.

I decided to remind Caren of what she had said to find out if anyone else agreed. She stumbled through her response. "I-I guess… I guess I've had different thoughts about that as we get closer to our trip to Glastonbury, and I don't know why, but it has put me on edge."

Three others simultaneously agreed, "Yes, me too."

"What's that all about?" Karin asked, twirling a lock of her hair.

"I don't know, but maybe it's the hike up that steep hill that the harpists want to take their harps to," I speculated. I wasn't certain if they even knew that possibility.

"What a hike, schlepping their precious harps all the way up there." Evelyn, a new participant, commented. "Has anyone seen pictures of the millions of steps to get to the top of that hill they call the Tor?" She asked.

Liz chimed in, saying, "Eeek, I get creeped out just seeing that Tor looming in the background when I watch some concerts from England; I don't want to research any part of it."

I was noting Liz's repulsed expression as Jill said in agreement, "I get a heavy feeling when I think of that place, and I haven't even been there yet."

"Well, this should be interesting," I said. We'll have to have "each other's six," as they say in fighter pilot action films or TV shows. I used to try spelling six-letter words that might fit in the six blanks, but the majority of the words were too short. I've got your back, your butt, your life, and then I figured it out.

I told them that it wasn't about words but about numbers on a clock. I explained that it means "behind you," as in the number six is on a clock, supposing everyone knows what a face clock is. The meaning of that phrase entails a very important commitment. "So let's have each other's back," I suggested.

The others who remained neutral, including the blowhard, Bob, listened with interest. As a show of support, they entered their fists into our circle and joined in our chant to each other as we raised our arms, "I've got your six."

For some strange reason, I was comforted by that brief ritual. The tension in the group had decreased exceedingly. With perfect timing, the class was letting out.

As we separated, there were more enthusiastic "See you tomorrows" than usual.

We were bonding, so perhaps more feedback will come out tomorrow. I was getting some kind of picture, but it was still slickly blurred.

"Hey." Cordelia greeted me with such enthusiasm that I knew we were going somewhere for supper.

I thought it would be fun to surprise her with what I surmised, so I asked, "So, where are we going tonight?"

"Did your group talk about it already? Bummer. I wanted the pleasure of surprising you. It's going to be so fun, don't you think?"

I was having a déjà vu moment from when I was in total darkness. I had struggled with similar questions on the phone with Cordelia back home: Where were we going? What would we be doing?

And why was she so animated? As with the last time, when I turned down the phone volume too low, and now when I acted like I knew everything, I had to give an admonition: "Cordelia, slow down; I have no idea what you're talking about. I was just trying to second-guess you, and it backfired badly."

"Oh, I figured someone in your group had heard about our group's plans—we wanted to go to a karaoke restaurant, wouldn't that be cool?" She responded.

"Don't you and your harpist friends have more than enough music every day? Wouldn't that be overkill?"

Cordelia explained thoughtfully, "Our harp playing is spiritual and reflective; it's about healing," before ramping it up, "But Karaoke is jammin' man, pure outright rockin'."

She had me there. I absolutely love karaoke. I have a favorite song I sing that takes the house down. It is by Four Non-Blonds and is called "What's Up?" It mentions several struggles I've had, leading to my "feeling a little peculiar," but there is a more meaningful part. I really ham it up when I get to the question, "What's going on?" I shake my pleading hand, look upward, and sing with authority, "Hey, hey, hey, what's going on?" as if I am demanding an answer. Little did I know I would be doing this very thing within a couple of days.

"So, what do you think?" Cordelia asked, tapping me on the shoulder. Huh? Should we go? Shall we join them?" By this point, she was dancing around and clinging to my arm.

When she heard my "yes," she broke into "Mustang Sally," which was probably her karaoke song choice. This is going to be great. I can hardly wait.

CHAPTER 16

Karaoke Anyone?

"THANK THE universe that the Karaoke Bar is in the same location as when we went out to eat a week ago, so it will be easy to find," said Cordelia reassuringly.

"Remember, we just walk out of here, down Lemon Street, and it's called the Longstore, across from Fairmantle Street." Cordelia has a good memory. I guess she'd need an excellent memory to remember all those notes, chords, and songs for the purpose of healing.

Cordelia was overwhelmed when we walked in the doorway. "Whoa, there's a lot more people here than the last time; are we going to sing in front of all of these people?"

"We're not going to be singing at all if we don't hurry and sign up for our song. Will you be doing the song you were singing earlier? What was it called?"

"I was going to sing 'Mustang Sally,' but now I'm not sure; there are a lot of people here," she replied.

"Well, let's sign up first and see how others do, then we'll confirm it among ourselves," I proposed, adding, "I'm also hungry, and I've been looking around for food but haven't found any; that's not going to be good."

Ever the sharp-eyed one, Cordelia said above the din, "I saw more people in the other room standing in a line with plates and napkin-wrapped silverware; we should go check that out," she said.

I put the proverbial "stick in the spokes" and said, "But first, we're going to find the place where we sign up for the karaoke."

She groaned, "Okay."

We located the person who would secure our position and songs. I smiled when I heard Cordelia request "Mustang Sally." The lady looked at me curiously when I proudly announced I would be singing "What's Up."

Turning to Cordelia, I said, "Okay, lead the way."

I followed her, weaving through the crowds this way and that, until we saw the end of the line, where we could arm ourselves with plates and eating implements.

I always get conflicted at buffet lines. I'm left-handed, so I need to serve myself from the right side of the steam table. In a study I did, it might be interesting to discover that the right-handed servers are opposite the left-handed diners.As usual, we had to wait for more of the meatballs, more of the potatoes, and more of the stuffed mushrooms. There were plenty of green beans.We knew we had about one-half hour before the karaoke began, but we were signed up so we could take our time eating. As I was looking around, I spotted Karin.

Cordelia noticed me waving to someone, and I said, "Oh, there is Cyndy, cool."

I remembered Karin speaking of Cyndy's reaction to the sad energy. When she reported that it gave them a sense of hopelessness, I recalled thinking that the boys who were going off to war with little hope of returning must have exuded that kind of energy.

As Cyndy and Karin lined up to fill their plates and we were ready to find a table, Cordelia shouldered her way to their place in line and said, "We'll save a seat for you at our table."

Cyndy smiled, nodding her head to acknowledge that she'd heard Cordelia."Now to find a place after I invited them to sit with us," Cordelia said, adding, "We've got to find an empty four-chair table; do you see any?"

"Over there," I replied, tilting my head in the direction I was indicating. "I think those people at that table are getting ready to leave; they've finished their dessert. It would be really rude for them to think they could sit back and just visit."

Cordelia laughed. "Your gift of people-watching may be paying off for us here; look, you were right, they're leaving; let's get over there."

We swiftly shuffled over to grab the table. "Ah, good to sit," I sighed with a breath of relief.

Cordelia stood up and waved for our new friends to see where we were seated.

As they approached, we made room on our table. "Hi, have a seat," I said as I introduced Karin to Cordelia. After the proper introductions were made, we began eating our tasty selections, and silence ensued.

"So, do you think we'll be playing our harps on the labyrinth?" said, breaking the silence.

Cyndy laughed. "I was just about to ask you the same thing," she said, adding, "but I've got a sketchy feeling about the whole thing, the whole trip."

"I agree," but say. "I get terrible inner tremors whenever I think about it."

"You too?" Karin asked as she leaned forward. "What could it be that's causing pauses in my head?"

Cordelia saw this as an opportunity to shift the conversation to an equally tenuous topic by asking, "So, did either of you sign up to sing?"

Ironically, someone was belting out Elton John's "Bennie and the Jets," and it sounded pretty good too. I was wondering if Cordelia was looking for support in order to avoid having to perform, but she wouldn't find any.

Looking at an excited Karin, Cyndy said, "I think Karin is doing 'Girls Just Wanna Have Fun' by Cyndi Lauper."

There were a lot of "oohs" and "ahhhs" from our side of the table.

Cyndy continued hesitantly, "But I'm not sure about me singing."

CHAPTER 17

....

Bam Bam

CORDELIA SMILED, directing her words toward me, "See, she doesn't want to do it either."

Both Karin and I simultaneously wailed, "Come on."

Karin was so strong in her protest, and I was surprised by what she said next: "Cordelia, not you too; Cyndy and I have been through this already, but I did get her to agree to sign up." In staccato, she added, "You two are not going to let us be the only ones going up there."

She was really pouring it on as she continued, "You will have to play your harps in front of strangers in a hospital or nursing home, so you might as well get over your stage fright tonight, in this place with your dear friends."Cordelia sheepishly laughed. "But we will never be playing in front of two jam-packed rooms."

I looked toward Cyndy. "I'm doing 'What's Up' by Four Non Blondes; so, what did you have in mind?" I was hoping that having to announce the song name would persuade her to join us.

"I signed up for Cher's 'Gypsys, Tramps, and Thieves' but I don't know," she replied.

For more encouragement, I continued, "Oh, I love that one; it will be good to hear it in a new rendition."

I was wearing her down. "Oh, alright. But... only if Cordelia will commit," she said.

Cordelia buckled under pressure, saying, "Okay, the non-harpists win." The two of them grabbed each other's arms, declaring, "We'll do it."

We tore the house down. When Cordelia got up to sing "Mustang Sally," the entire room was standing, swinging, and swaying, and her shakiness was obscured. They had just sat down to reconvene their chatting and drinking when I appeared on the little stage. All movement came to a halt, and ice cubes rattled into place to settle where the drinks were set down. It was as if they'd never heard "What's Up" performed before, at least not in my style. They cracked up when I lowered myself to one knee with the verses, "And I pray, oh, I pray to the saints all day for a revolution." They raised their arms in the pleading tone of my singing as I continued, "Hey, hey, what's going on?" They even joined in when encouraged.Cyndy was up next, and she had them standing. Couples were twirling arm-in-arm on their dancin' feet to her "Gypsys, Tramps, and Thieves." And lastly, it was the women who joined Karin in singing "Girls just wanna have fun." It became a bit riotous when they kept singing the chant even after the music stopped.

They toned it down when the next karaoke singer got up on stage. They must have been thinking, "What an act or acts to follow," but the guy persevered and did not disappoint with "Rockin' Robin" by Bobby Day. As the song suggests, we were a'rockin' plenty.

What a great night! Tomorrow would hold the answer to the quandary of whether they would bring their harps. It would reveal the answer to why there were chills when anticipating the Glastonbury trip. And yet the images seemed light-years away.

We had invited Karin and Cyndy to ride along with us, which was a nice change. Karin had seized the opportunity to delegate the driving to someone else. I had said I might drive this jaunt, but that wasn't happening.

For some reason, I felt I needed to steady myself for something unanticipated; although I'd anticipated something, I just didn't know what. The object of anxiety was always cloaked in some cold darkness.

When I saw Karin and Cordelia empty-handed, I deduced that they'd decided to forgo the harp ceremony. "So, no go on the harp?"

Cordelia explained that the alleged labyrinth is at the top of Glastonbury Tor and reportedly makes its way down the decline in a labyrinthine manner. She said that this place is the source of several myths, with stories of ceremonies carried on during King Arthur's time.

Cyndy jumped in and said, "We have no idea if the labyrinth really exists or whether it has been maintained or groomed to make it easy to follow, so we will leave our harps here since none of us wants to get our hopes up only to be disappointed."Cordelia said, sounding anxious, "Well, let's fasten our seatbelts and get this show on the road." Four snaps, and we were off. The extended presence of the fluffy Mary energy seemed to calm us all.

Everyone was reflective, but it was a comfy quiet. The ride through the Mary ley line was delicious, as we floated on a fluffy, refreshing, and renewing energy. We had been told there was quite a difference in the feel of the Mary line as opposed to the Michael line. The Mary line did not disappoint.

Swiveling my torso and head slightly so that I could connect with our friends, I announced, "The sweet feeling you are experiencing is from the energy of the Mary ley line that runs alongside another harsher energy called the Michael line, and we will know when we hit the latter."

Fortunately, they'd heard of ley lines, so I didn't have to worry about explaining what they are. They admitted they'd never knowingly experienced the energy of either the Mary or Michael lines. They did agree that they were enjoying the soft sensation Mary showered them with. For me, the feeling helped my mental anguish melt.

Just as the energy felt light, our conversation was light. Then, bam! bam!, Michael hit us and hit us hard.

CHAPTER 18

A Chilling Sight

"OOF, MY head is feeling funny, and my goodness, the pressure is almost unbearable," I said. I'm getting a severe headache, so I requested that Madeline do a dowse to see if I have entities.I explained to Cyndy and Karin that entities are spirit beings, not of deceased humans or animals, but something else altogether; something we don't understand, but we'd know when our soul is being interfered with.

They cause confusion and lack of focus and tamper with our physical, emotional, psychological, mental, or spiritual levels. Right now, Cordelia feels like she's been affected physically, so I explained, "I will dowse to see if she does have entities, and if she does, I will clear those entities and negative energies, which means I will neutralize or remove them."

"Oh, no, I wonder if I have those things too because my head feels like it's in a vice," Cyndy stated.

"Neither you nor Cordelia have entities," I remarked, and I wondered. . . I looked up through the windshield, or "windscreen," as it is called in England, and I fixed my eyes on one of the causes of our massive discomfort.

Karin asked, "What is that?" as she followed my gaze.

Everyone's attention was drawn to it as it menacingly reared its ugly head over the entire landscape. Large raindrops splatting our view and distorting its shape added to the drama in our car. Windshield wipers echoed a word, phrase or story in the gray gloom.

"That, my ladies, is the famous Glastonbury Tor of around five hundred-plus feet high," I said, adding "As it overshadows all thoughts we may have, it warns us that we are nearing the village of Glastonbury.

Karin spoke up, "Now, I have a crampy gut; what is going on?"

Just as I was about to smugly declare that neither the Michael ley line nor the vision of the Glastonbury Tor had affected me, I felt like I'd been clubbed in the back of my head and was being held down.

We talked about how we thought we'd left the Mary line and were now trudging through the Michael line.

I had been thinking about why this was happening and decided to throw it out to the group, saying, "I'm wondering if this is like the movie 'Close Encounters,' where people who were somehow connected were pulled to the same location to experience the energies summoning them there."

All eyes were glued on the impending figure as they intently considered my words. "This is a stretch, but maybe we were together in a past life, and that's why we're here, even in this car together," I speculated.

We didn't understand why we perceived it through a dark and emotional lens, but we will get our answer. I shared some of my previous research, saying, "The books said the Tor was dedicated to St. Michael the Archangel, a warrior against powers of darkness." Wow, the Michael line equals darkness. We were unaware of how much we were going to need St. Michael by our side.

I didn't know if the term torus was related to what we were experiencing, but there seemed to be a close connection. A torus flows in infinite directions, both up, down, and all around, simultaneously.

The whole area of the torus is an electromagnetic field. The Glastonbury Tor, a giant hill, consumed our attention as we drove toward it.

We were compelled to question the object jutting from the top central point. This area we were heading toward has been called the "Land of the Dead." I declined the opportunity to enlighten my already frazzled companions.

It may have been the effects of overexposure or my dowsing, but eventually, those sensations dissipated. That was a good thing, because we could not have endured such harsh energy for very long. We had no idea we'd be plunged into the roils of this energy so soon.

To change the topic, I decided to explore people's reactions or awareness to the harp chord demonstration. "I never got to ask people how they were affected by the various harp chords that were played for us as we observed the lady lying on the floor," I said.

Karin chimed in patting her harpist friend on the arm, "Oh, yuh, that was so cool, wasn't it?

It helped me understand of what Cyndy is learning."In an afterthought, she added,

"Oh, that's right, Madeline, you and I were going to exchange a summary of our responses, but we never found the time or opportunity."

Cyndy noticed that no one was directly answering Madeline's question, so she said, "I found myself having the opposite reaction to Janet, lying on the floor."

"It was weird; when she claimed that she felt relaxed, I was depressed; when she was agitated, I felt energized," Cordelia commented.

Karin said, trailing off, "I noticed I was feeling very peaceful when... what was her name?"

"Janet," Cyndi said.

Karin continued, "Oh yuh, so, as I was saying, I experienced peace when Janet reported feeling depressed."

I tied it all together with a cheerful note. That's cool; we all had the same reaction. I did notice many had similar responses to the way the chords sounded as Janet did. It must be something in the brain.

It was Cordelia, our chauffeur's turn, to pose a question: "Well, we're nearing the town of Glastonbury; should we just go straight to the Tor or down into town?"

We voted to go for it and head up to the Tor. Then the comments began to pour in as if a floodgate had been opened.

Cyndy was the first to emote. "Ugh, I've got the chills. Does anyone else see the darkness cloaking the individuals in this town? Every one of them."

"I know," I said. Every face is distorted and is looking right at us. There's something icky about this place.Cordelia was extremely affected. "What is with this place? Everyone's body is twisted, and they are moving in slow motion."

Karin's reaction was no different. "Everyone's aura is pea green, a sign of great sickness. It's either physical, or spiritual, or both, or on more levels. All I know is that it is putrid."

To find something redeeming to say, I pointed out that there were many shops about healing.

"Oh, I see what you mean," said Cyndy, pointing them out as we passed them.

Cordelia shared her ruminating thoughts. "It's as if something unforgiving occurred in this town, and it has never quite come back from it. Oh no."

When we looked at the sign on the sawhorse blocking our path, we understood why Cordelia had groaned.

Karin read the sign out loud. "Go no farther, turn around, and catch the shuttle bus in town to return to the Tor."

I couldn't help myself. "Whaaat? We have to go back down through that dark distortion of slimy sickness. I'm dowsing each of us a shield of protection."

CHAPTER 19

• • • • • • • • • • • • • • • •

The Spiritual Gauntlet

WE MADE it through the spiritual gauntlet, basically unscathed. The myriad of cars parked diagonally distracted me from really seeing my surroundings. I saw a sign indicating we had arrived at the shuttle-waiting line.

I watched Cyndy and Karin vanish through some door, obscured by a line of people. There was a wall of expansive writing on the building that caught Cordelia's and my curiosity.

When we got closer, we realized it was a written record of the history of the frail, rudimentary remnants of the Abbey or Monastery we were standing in front of. As Cordelia studied the message, she said, "We were here."

She continued to say, "This is the location of the ancient ruins of the violent destruction of the Benedictine Abbey during the 15th century."

My vision and hearing began to waver as she got to the words: "In the 15th century, the abbots were taken to the Tor and hung to their deaths. The chief, Abbot Richard, was buried at the top of the Tor.

As I took my last breath, standing there, I barely heard her voice as the words on the wall blurred and swirled.

There was such a loud buzzing in my ears that I did not hear her announce the most important part for me. "With no leadership present, the monastery was attacked and every monk, beheaded."

Distracted with confusion, I nearly collided with a heavy-set gentleman attempting to slide by me to access the same building Cyndy and Karin had entered. As I stepped aside, Cordelia's words rang in my ears, "We were here, we were here." Then...

I stepped down into darkness.

Had I been blinded by something or someone? Had we both been abducted and drugged? I could see nothing. My last memory was that we were standing outside some building waiting for the shuttle to take us up to the Glastonbury Tor in England.

Wherever I was, it was midnight-dark. There were neither windows nor skylights. It was, as my friend Marty used to say, "Darker than the inside of your pocket."

I felt around to get some clue as to where I was. The walls were made of large stones. I could feel their rough texture, and by the shape of them, I was quite certain they were mere fieldstones.

Swishing my hands around, I traced a rough stone floor, perceiving nothing to have been polished or smoothed. I rubbed my eyes to see anything, maybe to cause this frightening world to disappear and the world I knew, to reappear.

Toes wiggling freely, my feet seemed different and sensitive to a draft coming from somewhere. While I was bent over testing the floor's makeup, I blindly traced my feet.

Trembling fingers walked up the arch of my foot to a strap that had the consistency of leather. I timidly touched the other toes. The lavender Asics running shoes I wore every day were missing; my toes were bare and cold to the touch.

In order to check out my feet, I had to slightly lift some thick, weighty material. As I examined the fiber type, I was shocked to discover it cloaked my entire body, right down to my foot covering that had morphed into sandals. I had sandals on and a long, course skirt that nearly reached the rock-formed floor.

I heard feet pounding like giants—or maybe it was just the thump of my own heart. Deathly silence surrounded me, and I sensed I would find no source of noise outside that room. I heard no screams of pain. This encouraged me to think I was not in some kind of torture chamber.

As my eyes adjusted to the darkness, it was of little help. I felt what must have been my necklace, but it was tied around my waist. I have no idea why it would be there rather than gracing my neck. I must have had a rip-roarin' night wherever I was.

But I had no alcohol to drink at karaoke. In fact, when some enthusiastic guy yelled, "I want what she's drinking," I wanted to yell, "It's a glass of ice." I said nothing and secretly enjoyed my ice cubes over ice.

Patting my pocket area, I dared plunge into the depths of some "gimundous"-sized pockets. Sometimes, like a lady's purse, one could find out a lot about someone by checking their pockets. Maybe I could discover more about the person whose clothes I was dressed in.

Hmm, no money. Hopefully, my fanny pack was somewhere in that room. Huh, the only thing I found was a bracelet of tiny beads.

As I was spinning around in the corner of this claustrophobic room, I stubbed my toe and slammed my shin into something sharp. The pain of injured toes is bad enough, but I've always considered my shin to be my proverbial Achilles' heel. This seemed to be a striking foreshadowing. Not good.

I sidled along the injurious object. Using a pacing measurement, I judged the knee-high mass to be about six feet long. When testing the width, I speculated that it was some sort of low table. But there were no expected objects on it, such as a book or magazines, or in this case, a simple candle with matches or a cigarette lighter. I altered my assessment. It may not have been a table but a bed with a thin, scratchy wool blanket, like the old army blankets.

CHAPTER 20

Stark Truth

IT WAS time to "bite the bullet" and test it out. If this unidentifiable object was unable to support me, at least I didn't have far to fall.

I tentatively lowered myself as one would employ a block and tackle pulley. As my heavily padded butt made contact with the surface, I didn't sense any "memory foam mattress top" comfort. It was a board.

Resting my entire body upon this tentative support, with my shaky elbows on trembling knees, I knew I had to figure out what was going on, where I was, and even more importantly, where Cordelia was being held.

Was my dear friend lying on a rough piece of plywood in another frigid room with no light, wondering where she was or where I had been swallowed up? It was my greatest hope that she was still outside in the light; worried someone had abducted me.

I had to get out of that room to explore further. I'd groped around the walls and the air, hoping to detect a switch or pullstring. There was no evidence of light switches, lamps, or candles.

I had estimated where the doorway would be and did the "Tim Conway shuffle" until I could feel a broadening of breathing space. Even the silence echoed through a long hallway. We must have been kept underground. There was the weak glow of a wall lantern guiding me.

As I continued tracing more stone walls along a widening corridor, my detective-like instinct caused me to question more intently where I was and what this place was.

I was brought back to the present moment. At least I thought it was the present moment. A bell was clanging somewhere within one of the adjoining reverberating rooms.

I headed out with determination to find its source, but my reconnaissance mission was rudely interrupted by a male voice: "Brother Samuel, you are late for prayer. See me after, for your penance."

Since his rebuke was directed toward me, I glanced down the corridor I'd just tip-toed up, with throbbing toes and shins. There was no one there in the shimmering shadows.

I had no idea who he was or who Brother Samuel was. He spoke with authority. I had the feeling I'd better find where the others were for this prayer, which I was allegedly tardy for.

I hoped that following the sound trail of the bell would lead me to where others were and where I was supposed to be.

Fortunately, for some reason, everyone was lying on their stomachs. Copying them, I placed myself in the same position on the gray and cold stone floor. I immediately experienced great discomfort.

I did not have to struggle, as one might expect, with how to adjust my breasts to the icy stone. I would either need to tuck and tape as the drag queens do or find an athletic cup. I was no longer a woman.

This new way of life was just not going to work out. I planned to pull someone aside and ask them what they do. One of my friends, who was a nun, had given me valuable information about their habits or dresses.

I can already hear Sister Barbara, who became just "Barbara," correcting me about how everyone mistakenly uses the word "nun" for someone who is in an active community. They were teachers who could leave their convent, unlike the Benedictine monks.

When my friends and I occasionally visited a group in Vermont, not more than an hour away, we observed that they wore thick black robes, with the exception of "newbies," known as Novices, who wore white robes.

Barbara told me that the cloth her habit was made of was five yards of serge, a thick, heavy material. That, I believe, was what was keeping me warm.

Where there was sufficient light, I looked at just what I was wearing. I don't know if it was to my advantage or not, but I was wearing white.

Monks spoke only of necessity. Well, it was of necessity for me to find out what the other guys do with their bulky protrusion, I referred to as a "unit. "

Something was going to have to be done about this torture on these rolling, solid bubbles for a floor. My worst fear was that they would tell me, "It is part of the deal." What if they say, "You'll get used to it"? What shall I ever do, then?

I was fortunate to hear one of the other men address my punisher as Abbott Richard. He seemed to be the superior here. I think they are called "Priors."I soon found out what penance was. Abbott Richard said, "Stand ready at the chapel door for the day and report one hour before the others for each hour for prayer."

I was told that if I had to relieve myself, I was granted permission to do so and to immediately return to carry out my penance. I was reminded that prayer times were three hours apart.

I counted myself fortunate because I didn't have to lie prostate, I mean prostrate on that cold floor all day. I hoped I would never commit any "No… no's" to warrant that.

Later, I did see an occasional brother spending the entire day lying face-down in the discomfort of rough stone. I didn't want my mind to go working to figure out or begin to imagine what he must have done to warrant that penance, or even who it was, in case it was one of my present-day friends.

CHAPTER 21

Wearing White

I DIDN'T know much about male anatomy, even though I was now the onus of said member. I couldn't help but wonder if lying prostrate on a cold floor causes the prostate problems I had heard of.

There was too much similarity in the words, "prostrate, prostate." I'd heard the warning that if you sit on a cold stone, you could get piles, whatever those are.

I just hoped none of the penances doled out involved sitting on that floor. I certainly did not want piles added to these other attached inconveniences. Maybe standing was the lesser of the two evils.

Standing sounds like a breeze, but it's not. After a while, I had to cheat and touch the doorway frame so as not to topple over. I was clearly listing, and I was fortunate no one was nearby to see how weak I was. One of the consolations was the delightful wafting of incense that permeated the chapel. I would eventually come to realize that the fragrance of myrrh served several functions. It aids in prayer and ritual.

Probably more importantly, a mere amount of comfort was allotted. It masked male hormones, sweat, unbathed bodies, and unlaundered frocks.

I thought it would be a relief to be able to move when I had reason to relieve myself. Not so. I had been standing so long that I think my knees were locked, and my hips forgot how to move. The pain felt like angry pins were being driven into my joints.

I wasn't sure I could make it down the stairs, and pulling myself back up was worse. My body begged me to return to my quiet standing position. I was able to hobble in to kneel and sit with the others. But when I wasn't joining in some prayer ritual or eating, I was a soldier standing at the ready.

When the group did arrive, I straightened up to create the illusion that it was "no problem" to have received this penance. No one seemed very interested in my standing there.

I was sure others had received the same consequence; there couldn't be that many original means of torture. They knew why I was there and that I was posing and pulling myself up to stand as erect as I could, with great effort.

Something strange is happening to my mind, and, I must say, it is very terrifying. I'm beginning to know things about the new me, or, should I say, the old me, the 15th century, Middle Ages me.

I'm wearing white because I am a Novice. We are learning about the Benedictine rule. St. Benedict believed idleness to be the enemy of the soul. It sounds like the time-worn saying or sayings, "Idleness is the devil's workshop, or playground, or worse yet, the root of all evil." Clearly, Benedict was banning any workshops or playgrounds for the devil. He established a horrid horarium, throughout which, I am being disciplined for showing up tardy for prayer. I have stepped through a vortex and arrived in the 16th century at the 3 p.m. prayer known as None.

Abbot Benedict had a favorite chant, which, as I can see, is not about having fun. It is actually about having no fun. "Ora et Labora" means prayer and work. Our schedule, or horarium, is strictly arranged, so there is no time for recreation or enjoyment. He arranged it so there are three hours between every activity—sleeping, working, eating, and praying—in no particular order.

It is no wonder that the picture on the plate we used for our biscuits in our little cottage, was a "trigger." I think Cordelia arranged for me to be spared having to wash it. I know she rigged the coin toss when we were flipping to see who would be designated to touch that chill-producing biscuit holder.

This guy, Benedict, made it nearly impossible for us to enjoy ourselves. Imagine me, the group comedian, having to refrain from jokes or laughter. How will I ever relate to these people?

Thus far, I've not uttered a word. I wonder if I speak in an English dialect, and if so, in what part of England? I'm at a slight disadvantage with my long-term amnesia.

I have no inkling who I am, why I'm here, or where I'm from. I have so many questions. Do I have a family? Are there people out there who care about me? What will happen if I see them and don't recognize them?

I needn't have worried about finding myself in such an awkward situation. We were forbidden to speak to anyone except in the case of a business transaction, reassuring the donor that we were doing penance and praying for their intentions.

At times, we were to collect donations from prayer petitioners. We could, without consequence, converse briefly and politely with the parents of our brothers, but never with our own parents.

To be permitted to speak with any one of the brothers but their own offspring—what must that have done to tear their hearts asunder?

CHAPTER 22

Teeter Totter

I GUESS my Brothers are content to just chalk it up to more daily penance, whereas our parents did not realize the yanking and pulling at their hearts they would be called to merely volunteer for.

Our tormented loved ones gain some ground in these incidents by being consoled in the belief that they are making our lives easier. A parent must often sense, just on the other side of the wall, the energy of the physical presence of their loved one, whom they surrendered to God for His work here on earth. To endure this, they hold onto the hope of being rewarded with an honorary place in what they believe to be the Kingdom of Heaven.

Working outside, we had to quickly gobble up any gifted sweet biscuit or other delicacy. The "do-gooder" knew. Flipping us a penny or two would neither be satisfying nor gratifying.

I think they often felt sorry for us. I certainly feel sorry for us. These men of the medieval times didn't have the knowledge that what they had to endure would one day be highly discouraged and would yield much less fortune.

I recently heard the completion of the saying, "Ignorance is bliss." They said, "Then knowledge is pain," thus my distaste for these times. Money was useless to us. But by-passers desiring to express the gratitude they feel for our doing penance for their prayer intentions will sometimes put us in unsafe situations. To see if we may have acquired something sweet from a passer-by as a little treat, our closet area and beds are randomly searched.It would be to our greatest well-being that only our cowl, tunic, sandals, shoes, belt, knife, stylus, needle, handkerchief, and writing tablets ever be found there.

If anything is found, we will be severely punished. This would render a far worse consequence than my having to stand the near full twenty-four hours of one day, when first being shuttled back into this sample of Hell.

I was slowly memorizing some of the Brothers' names. One that I especially felt concern for was named Zachary. I was sensing a brittleness in his psyche as I observed his cheek muscles twitch. He was on my mind a lot. I sent him healing on all levels. I just felt he needed some kind of shield of protection.

Rather than yielding clarity to the cause of his morosity, the next incident only increased my bemusement. One morning at Matins, Brother Zachary's prayer bench was empty. There was no lovely, prayerful, contemplative chanting coming from his chapel corner.

As our group moved on into the refectory or dining room, each taking our designated chair and place at the table, I was further befuddled. Not only was Zachary missing at the table but so was his place at the table. It was as if he were never there, never existed.

There was no sign he'd ever been there. The two Novices who had flanked him now sat beside each other. No one ever spoke of it.

I don't know if maybe he was punished so severely for disobeying some Benedictine rule. What could any Brother do that is so non-negotiable that his violation warranted expulsion?

Someone made an example of him to serve as a frightening deterrent against any similar violation of the rule. I will leave it there; enough said, except… He was not just an illusion. He isn't a figment of my imagination. I will miss his comforting alto voice.

To continue the topic of accruing money for penance, I began to understand how the Vatican has become financially secure. It originated with us. As our monastery's "fan-base" grew, it became richer.

Some might think we would have more comfort, better food, actual metal forks and metal spoons, and metal knives to cut into rich red meat or even chicken or pork.

It doesn't change our way of life, though. It is our harsh schedule that makes the money—the more brutal, the more valuable and lucrative we are.

The monks benefit nothing, for to have better food, better eating utensils, and better beds would undo the reason the church monastery makes the money, which, I'm sure, eventually ends up in Rome.

There is a Catch-22 here, because the church monastery made or still makes money as a result of us monks. There must always be hardships and penance.

If we had more comfortable beds, it would become a double-edged sword for those who benefit from the profits.It is a bit like a teeter-totter with the church monastery on one end and the monks on the opposite end. The degree to which the monks suffer is in direct relationship to the measure of profits.

Abbot Richard ran a tight ship. I wonder if he was schooled by Benedict himself—the one who started all of this.

I do have to speak in his favor. He never asked or demanded that we do anything he did not practice himself. There was even one act of daily penance he carried out, but he left it up to our discrepancy. He said, to my relief, "The wearing of a hair shirt is between you and your God."

I am sure my God knows how freaked out I get when I am trimming my hair and some of the tiniest of hairs get on my neck and/or shirt.

There seems to be no relief, no way to get those prickly little needles out of the material or separated from my skin.

I am certain, all things considered, that my God would not ask me to wear a shirt of coarse material made of goats' hair—something that would continuously irritate and agitate my bare skin.

No, he would never ask that of me, especially since I did not knowingly sign up for this magical mystery tour through the godforsaken 16th century. I have no idea how long until my ticket expires, before my stay here is terminated.

CHAPTER 23

Whaat No Coffee?

THE REFECTORY or dining room is one of the places where those lay people requesting prayers, if allowed inside our hallowed stone walls, would be able to make the assumption that the height of our difficulty may be partaking of meals.

I see a wooden plate at my designated place at the table in the refectory as I sit down for supper. Whaaat no coffee? There is hot water for some herbal tea looking like wet seaweed, in my wooden cup.

Only the crackle of the wood in the fireplace, wood scraping against wood, and a monotoned reader could be heard. There is occasional slurping.No worry of criticism for bad manners as I grab a chunk of the loaf of acorn bread passed to me. I hesitate to eat it; acorns are so bitter-tasting, but so is this life. Surprisingly, the bread tastes fine.I never would have anticipated our eating equipment. I won't call them utensils because that denotes metal. It was as if they only had the large kitchen cooking forks and spoons for us to use to consume our food.I've read that if we are attracted to or repulsed by something, such as a culture, artwork, music, stories, or movies about a particular era, event, or person, we are possibly connecting to a past-life experience. I think I have found the reason for my aversion to wet wood.

It gives me the "heebie-jeebies." As a child in the 1950s, whenever I finished eating a popsicle or fudgesicle, I had to clean the wooden stick off with my teeth while avoiding any touch of the tongue.

I wonder about people who scrape their teeth across their metal, stainless steel forks as they eat, shaping ridges on their top teeth. Are they still practicing that same defense in this lifetime, giving me more chills?What am I to do with giant wooden spoons and giant wooden forks as tools for eating vegetables, vegetable soups, yummy gruel, or eggs of every sort on slimy, slippery wood?

All along, one of the senior brothers, reading from none other than "The Rule of St. Benedict," has been droning us.

This is one of Benedict's methods to dull the senses—never to have a private moment. The food isn't anything we'd want to savor anyway, in case that was one of his aims.

I use the time to study who everyone is and who they might have been reincarnated as in the 20th century. I think I have figured a few out.

I'm jolted back into reality when I feel a familiar tapping on my shoulder. That's the way Cordelia always brings me back from my mental wanderings. It made me miss her more.It is Brother Stephen on his knees. When I look into his bright, alert eyes, I know, through my inner dowsing—recognizing his soul—that he would eventually be reborn into the 20thcentury in the United States as a girl named Cordelia, who would become my dear friend.

I miss her so much.

I know I'll soon be going from brother to brother, just as he is, in a most humiliating posture, kneeling, whispering, "Please, Brother, may I have some food?."

A weird feeling washes over me, surging through me—embarrassed for Stephen and extremely humiliated and irritated at being asked for food. I guess this is just one more act of penance.I'm obviously not supposed to be enjoying my meal anyway. Heaven forbid that happens. I guess we were to take sustenance those nights from "shame soup." When the reading from the section of The Rule of Benedict is completed, there is absolute silence, except for the knocking of wooden forks or wooden spoons against wooden plates or bowls. Ewww. Wet wood. When I, in the past, or should I say, "In the future" offered to wash friends' dishes, I didn't realize there was a surprise waiting for me. Dipping into the dishpan, my unsuspecting fingers made contact with several cooking spoons made of wood. My teeth would grind together with the same reaction people have to fingernails on a chalkboard. Although I'm uncertain about how many are able to relate to that analogy, I hope I never have to do dishes in this here-and-now monastery. It just might put me over the edge.

After an anticipated and truly disgusting supper, I was spared from wet wood-handling duty. Still, in penance, I had to high-tail it to stand in preparation for the evening prayer, Vespers.

As you can see, there weren't any extras for a little sweet treat. This is why I earlier spoke of how we would have to sneak stuff without getting caught. We just have to make sure we draw no closer than approximately five feet from Brother Richard, lest he smell sweetness on our breath or detect crumbs on our rosy cheeks.

Vespers are to quiet us down for the night. I don't know how much quieter we can be without becoming comatose. We chant some psalms from a prayer book. The material does not seem to have any substance. It's just more about the fighting among the Babylonians and whomever they are battling in said psalm. Barring the subject matter, the chanting is beautiful.

I'm not sure when we'll hit the sack, er, board. I will need to be at the entrance to the chapel for the 3 a.m. Lauds. This is not showing much sleep in my future. It turns out the darkened room you witnessed me "landing in" must have been a guest room of some sort, which explains why there was no candle. None of us sleep in a single room like that.

Rather, we all sleep in one large room, where each of us is doled out a woolen blanket, some lighter-weight cover, and a pillow on a mat-covered board, identical to the one I banged into, while searching the original room.

In an effort to prevent temptations, we must each sleep in our own bed, with a senior monk between any of us from the same set.

Furthermore, there is someone who supervises our sleeping as we lie there clothed, girded with belts or chords. If any have swords, they leave them at the door.

I guess the powers-that-be are afraid there might be fights. "No swords or knives in bed" might save some of us from accidentally running ourselves through with our own sword or knife. That would be cutting irony.

A lamp burns the entire night until morning's light. We are to be at the ready for any need to get up for the prayer hours I've told you about.

I'm uncertain if we will be allowed to return to our bed after the 3 a.m. Lauds. I suspect we will just meditate. It is believed to be more restful than R.E.M. sleep.

Another hop, skip, and a jump away and I will be expected to be the informal undesignated greeter at Prime at 6 a.m.

Lastly, I am to arrive one hour early for the 9 a.m. prayer, serving my penance, which is nearing its completion, just a few hours away. I can almost taste freedom.I promise I will never be late for prayer, ever.

CHAPTER 24

The Meeting

WE WILL be praying Terce at 9 a.m. I'm hoping some breakfast time is scheduled here. Eating didn't seem to be too important to Benedict. At noon, there's food for the soul with a prayer called Sect. Before that, we have to begin working outside. This is not showing much sleep in my future.

One of the monks, Patrick, disappears from the group during the time we are working outside. I can't figure it out. I've looked all around outside to spot him anywhere. There is no sign of him.

When I get outside, it is still warm. It is still summer. So, nothing funky has happened to the seasons in this major change of centuries. Stephen, Abraham, Francis, and I are to be cutting sheaths of grain. The land is marshy, but there was work done to drain it before I arrived.

I need to skip over to the little barn with Abraham to teach him how to milk the cows. He, fortunately, is a good student. It could have been a challenge, but, having learned from my grandparents as a kid at in the 1950s, I could easily teach my brothers.

Abraham draws a few of us aside, one at a time, to secretly listen to our problems and frustrations about living with the older brothers.

Some are courteous, but others act as if they believe we don't know what we are doing. The problem is that we can only be friends with those who came into the monastery at the same time we did.

Because they are not from our set, we never get to know anything about them, nor them about us; it doesn't make for the best working arrangements or environment.

When I had a rare moment, I scanned the area, but there was still no sign of the mystery man. I was quite sure it wasn't a "Zachary situation" because Patrick usually shows up a little early for all prayer times.

I've long ago abandoned the idea of asking anyone what to do for comfort while lying on the cold stone floor. I've resigned myself to discomfort. I see no sense in any of it, but I am here, so I will make the best of it, whatever that might look like.

I'm beginning to put together these Monks' names and who they became as my friends. Many of them are here. I've just got to find some private time. That may be when we are supposed to sleep.

I want to know who's here with me. I'm strangely comforted by the reassurance that I'm not alone. Peering into their eyes, my desperate isolation grows darker. I know it is their soul I recognize, but they have no idea who I am.

Having gone full circle, my penance will be fulfilled. I will finally be able to arrive for prayer at the regular hours. This will give me more thinking time. I've got to quickly jot down notes on my observations and speculations before they escape me.

I was figuring I'd have to meet with our Prior. Sure enough, Brother Richard caught me in the same spot he originally confronted me on the day this 16th-century nightmare began.

Just outside, in the 21st-century, there is a large wall sign recording the cause and effect of the ruination of the Glastonbury Monastery. Ruins? What could have happened to turn this massive building into fallen, crumbled stone?

"Brother Samuel, your period of penance is complete. I will see you after None in my office."

Being dutiful, as soon as 3 p.m. prayers were completed, I headed down the corridor toward Prior Richard's sanctuary. I am reassured when Robert appears at prayer. There is no "Zachary disappearing" situation to cause concern.

I have only been down in this section where Richard has his office one other time. It was when I went to hear my penance for being late for prayer. I'm kind of nervous, worrying he will give me more penances.

As I dare raise my head, I catch a glimpse of who I think is Brother Sylvester. What would he be doing down here? I do not recall ever seeing him working outside with us, though.

When he walks in my direction, I confirm it is Sylvester, and he is carrying a leather-bound book that looks very much like a ledger.

My attention to what Sylvester is about is yanked away by that same male voice that startled me only a day ago, which seems like weeks ago. I might have thought months had passed if it weren't still summer.

Maybe in vortexes, time does bumps and jumps, because I've lost track of how much time I've been away from my 21st-century present-day friends. I wonder what they are doing.

Has the shuttle for the Tor arrived? Have they gone along anyway? Are they missing me? Have they found some authorities to begin searching for me?

"Brother Samuel, come into my office and have a seat," Prior Richard said, as he motions for me to enter. It all comes back to me, roiling and rearing desperate waves of panic. I can't move. Prior Richard gives me an unnerving stare, not soft but hard, drilling right into my soul. I know if I do not move soon, it will appear as a refusal to obey.

He is gearing up to quietly bark that I am to kneel on the spot and get a penance.

My sandals are glued to the floor.

CHAPTER 25

Penance

COULD THIS be the root of my phobia of authority figures? Every time an employer says, "Can I see you?" or "We need to talk," I freeze up, expecting the worst.

And oftentimes, it indeed has been something to grip my pounding, chaotic heart. I've been "let go" or told I should consider moving on. Is that what will happen here?

Is it self-prophecy or fallout from my penance days? It makes sense. The horridly unfair sentence or the canonical, monastic word, penance, paralyzes me.

Has some sticky substance like honey been previously spilled on the stones below where I walk? Just a few steps farther, and I will make it to the rough wood bench I have been directed to. What will I do if I can't mentally unfasten my feet?

It's as if Sylvester somehow senses my terror. He passes conveniently near me, dropping his prayer beads. Without a word but a look, I snapped out of my fugue, give an assist, and went to retrieve them.As our eyes meet, I know what he is saying. There's a quirking at the corners of his mouth, strangling a smile. Sylvester is an inner dowser like Cordelia.It dawned on me that he would eventually be reborn in the 20th century in the United States as a girl named Somara. She would become a new, dear friend in the little time I was in England. I miss her laugh and her voice.

"Well, Brother Samuel, I do not have all day; aren't you here because you just served a penance for dallying, or do you need another one? Have you learned nothing, Brother?" Sylvester said as he rubbed the back of his neck.

I carry myself to the indicated bench as fast as my now-freed feet are able to follow each other. I am seated and silent. So is Prior Richard. I am sure I can see smoke seeping from orifices in his smoldering skull.

If I am dismissed or kicked out, where will I go in the 16th century? I know no one, nor am I remotely acquainted with these times. I don't think I even studied it in school.

I had uncomfortably taught this era to sixth graders, yet they remembered none of it. Here, I am finding many answers to questions I always had regarding the inner dialogue surfacing during those classroom discussions. As I stood in front of my students, unearthing that subject must have felt all too familiar.

I exhaled a sigh of resignation.

"Brother Samuel, because you wear a white robe, indicating you have a novice brain and soul, I will overlook what just happened; but you have been warned. When I address you, you are to kneel on the spot with your head lowered until you are given permission to raise it. Is that clear?"

I don't know if that was a rhetorical question and I'm expected to remain silent, or, on the other hand, should I speak with words of acknowledgment?

I choose the latter, but I am slammed with the realization that I do not know the appropriate way to respond. What do I call him?

I don't think "Sir, yes, Sir," would be correct, although the situation is very similar to that of the Army, or maybe more like the Marines.

I settled with, "Yes, Prior Richard"

"You may leave," he responded. As I raised myself from the bench, he continued, "And, Brother Samuel, I do not want to have to see you here again. Is that clear?"

With every inner organ trembling, I shakily bowed my head and said, "Yes, Prior Richard."

He gestures for me to scoot, and scoot I did, but not without signaling Brother Sylvester a "thank you" one more time. I put as many stones as I could as quickly as I could between me and that ominous ordeal.

When I had distanced myself enough from the trauma, my mind returned to wondering what it must have been like for Sylvester to have to examine and add to all those figures in that book. Hopefully, he is able to see them as just numbers and not as dollars and wealth as he returns to his board bed and boorish meals. I feel a special sadness for him and an affinity toward him.

I'm consoled to know he will fare much better than my new friend Somara in the 21st century as she works with someone else's accounts and concerns and happily returns to a warm, welcoming home with good cuisine, comfortable furniture, and a fine, cushy bed.

When did man's thoughts become so hardened? It is all dependent upon balance, and Sylvester replaced that in my soul today in the 16th century. But Somara has already done that many times for me in the 21st century.

When I put my hand in my pockets, I am reintroduced to a "little friend" I met on the first day in this monastery. Remember, I had thought it was a bracelet with a cross on it.

I am supposed to be using it many times a day; I think about eight times. We were told to say some prayers daily, asking for indulgences.

Indulgences are necessary as a way to reduce the amount of punishment we have to go through to pay for our sins.

It seems as though someone would have to invent sins in this place. We actually check with each other for ideas for sins to confess.

There is another session called Chapter of Faults, where we are told of some infraction someone may have committed. We are to kneel to acknowledge the offense.

If no one kneels because they are unaware they have done any such thing, about five of us from our set will "hit the floor" to bail the guilty brother out.

The other thing I have been unable to grasp is: why all this punishment and penance if God has already allegedly forgiven us? Didn't He have His Son die for our sins?

CHAPTER 26

····················

More Answers

THE OTHER useful information I have received is that the beads I thought were a necklace around my waist are the large version of the rosary.

For me, they served as a notification of who was walking toward me. I've gotten so good at it that I am able to identify a brother by how his beads rattle.

Everyone has a different stride; some are lanky, some are hurrying, and others are more graceful. This causes the rosary beads to click together differently for each brother.

It's nice to know who the brother is; I just want to know who some of these brothers will be. I have solved two, Stephen, who was begging for food, is Cordelia, and Sylvester is Somara.I've got a hunch that Robert is Karin, who becomes a psychiatrist. Even back in the 16th century, he was showing kindness beyond the call of duty.

He risks getting severely punished to help those who find they can trust him. I miss seeing Karin's smile. We've become quite close while she has been taking harp lessons in the 21st century.

I am getting confused about how to phrase things. Karin isn't here in the 16th century; Robert is. Neither Caren, Cyndy, Cordelia, Mary Jo, nor Somara, are taking harp lessons in this lifetime. They may not even know how to play the harp yet.

You'd think the longer I remained here, the less confused I'd be, but it seems to have only worsened matters. My head is like a closet with things just thoughtlessly thrown into it.

Working with the cows gives me time to ruminate over vital facts. My most comforting ol' girl is Alfalfa, who reminds me of a beloved calf on my grandparents' farm in my 20th-century childhood.

I need to find out where Patrick disappears every day. Is his activity legal? Does he leave the Monastery grounds, risking expulsion? Does his closeted behavior have Prior Richard's blessing? Is he safe?

It's not that I can do anything about it. I just have to know. I care about him, and I might know him from the 21st century. I hope I've timed things right today.

When I'm finished here, I'll rush the milk bucket to the kitchen bench, where I have been requested to leave it. Then, I'll slip back outside to watch for his return and track his route.

I used to love to shovel manure as a child at my grandparents'. I take a big inhale and am lifted away for a short time, reminiscing about those days. It occurs to me that this might be where I acquired a taste… er… attraction… affinity, for the "eau de parfum de manure." As I toss the last bit of manure onto the pile, I spot Patrick exiting a small, mysterious stone building—a kiddie corner—from where I am standing.

My bemused eyes follow him until he disappears into the monastery. Following my previous clandestine plan, I am back outside, playing hide and seek until I am safely back with my girls, the Jerseys, the brown-white patched cows.

If I could get to the back of that building, I could jimmy the door with a slab of wood, undetected. I have to get inside that building to see what he's been doing every day. There seem to be only one or two other senior-level brothers working with him.

I can conveniently dart to a hedge lined on the side closest to me and then quickly get the answers to my many questions. Continuing to carry out my project, I encounter one damned deterrent.

There is no rear entrance. There is one long stretch of stonework and no planked door. I have to risk entering through the front, exposed to everyone.

It occurs to me that there is little chance of anyone spying on me as I attempt to gain access to a forbidden area. Gambling with the security of my stay here will risk my expulsion.

Any windows in there are too high up from the floor for anyone to have the opportunity to peer out to see even a blue sky. This was one more of Benedict's monastic methods—to ensure further denial of the senses.

This time, one of his torturous inventions is going to favor me. My wooden wedge works well. The heavy door scrapes and creaks on its leather hinges. I am beside myself when I stick my head through the interior.

Throughout the time we have been at the cottages, she has gifted us with different lovely bowls. Each was a piece of pottery Caren had fashioned for the occasion, much like the ones lined up on the shelves I'm staring at in this 16th-century room.

I am now convinced that Patrick will eventually be reborn to the 20th-century United States as a girl named Caren to become a renowned potter. Joyously, I refasten the door and dance down the steps.

I catch myself in mid-air, returning to reality—how much time have I used? Being outside, I would miss the call for vespers. They may have already begun.

I cannot be late. We are not doing this again. I beg under my breath, "Please, please don't let me be late; don't let them have already started." Though running through the halls and corridors is forbidden, I hurriedly sashay toward the chapel. I almost faint on rubbery legs when I realize what I'm seeing.

There are at least five of my brothers entering the chapel. Either I'm saved or we are all doomed. I assume the usual prostrate position on the floor, hoping to create an impression of normalcy.

We return to our prayer benches and begin to chant the psalms. More "bashing Babylonian babies against the rocks" in Psalm 137:9.

"Blessed is he who seizes your infants and dashes them against the rocks. Happy is the one who seizes your infants and dashes them against the rocks."

During our short time preceding supper, I hurriedly jotted down my findings regarding Patrick. Oh, I'm excited now. I'm slowly finding everyone who is attending or accompanying participants in the harp therapy course of the 21st century.

People might be wondering why I care about who's who in the 16th century. I sometimes wonder too. I think at one time I knew why it matters, but it is all too quickly fading.

As I said earlier, when we were in the car, I wondered if some of this was like the movie "Close Encounters," where people who were somehow connected were pulled to the same location, in this case, the harp therapy course, to experience the energies summoning them there.

The common reactions to the Town of Glastonbury are a red flag for me. I had earlier thought it was a stretch, that maybe, we were in a past life together. The problem is that among us, I am the only one who has been to the future and has unwillingly returned to the past. I know I can't start talking to them about the future as if I've been there, like the talk heard on some science fiction show on television.

People do talk about recognizing someone they are sure was with them in a past life, but rarely speak about meeting them again in the future. I best not broach any such topic.

So here I am, forming strange friendships in the 16th century with people whom I have grown quite close to in a surprisingly short time in the 21st century.

CHAPTER 27

A Particular Friendship

THIS DAY, I am working with Justin, a senior brother, yet again. We are developing a nice relationship even though we aren't supposed to. Everyone else is tending to some other tasks.John is minding our five sheep. We'll eventually have to help him shear them for wool before he teaches us how to prepare clumps of their coats to be made into yarn.

With his skill using whale bones shaped like quills, there will be knitted cowls and capes and pairs of Coptic socks—a roughly shaped garment to fit the foot for thongs or sandals—for us. After that, he will gift us with yummy, warm mittens.

He's in good company. Several paintings that portray Mary, the mother of Jesus, were done while she was knitting. It was called The Knitting Madonnas.

It's something John must have learned here in the 16th century before entering the monastery. Funny, I don't think about each brother's past in this lifetime, having no idea of who they were, only their future lifetime.

I remember Cyndy in the 21st century telling me about heritage stories about sheep herding on her mother's side of the family. The maternal grandparents were from the Isle of Sheppey. I think it was also named Sheep Island. It seems like sheep herding runs in her blood.

Cyndy brought her knitting with her into the 21st century to knit mittens for her grandchildren. Those were easier to pack than the knitted blankets she's working on for them. She said it relaxed her to knit. She needed to keep those harp fingers limber.

I believe that John will eventually be reborn in the 21st century United States as a girl named Cyndy.Of course, Sylvester is inside, working on the books. Joseph is decorating the chapel, and Francis is tending the flowers for Joseph to place in specific areas in the chapel on Sundays and holy days. Now I know why Patrick is never on our work crew.

Abraham is off to the side "counseling" another brother whom I do not know well. I can't help but notice, watching the other brother's arms flail, that they are having a spirited exchange.

There must have been some issue that stirred him up. It's a good thing Abraham is around for us. We have someone we know who can be trusted and who makes no judgment.

I can't imagine how many rumbles there might be if he weren't here. Maybe this is why there are no swords or knives allowed near the beds. If pressure builds up too much…

They would definitely need James to attend to them. He seems to have knowledge of medicine, injuries, and healthy behaviors. I think Prior Richard has him stay inside in case any of us get injured or sick. Abraham is not going anywhere, as long as he doesn't get caught or reported. It is okay for brothers in the same set to talk in moderation, but I'm afraid this counseling every day while others cover for him would not be looked upon favorably.

That could mean a mass penance—everyone involved would be penanced. Hmmm. That would be everyone in our set. I shudder to imagine what that might amount to or look like.

I, too, am in denial about the risks I'm taking. I am just supposed to be silently working, basically disregarding the risk I'm taking to deepen my friendship with Justin, who is in the set a year ahead of me.

I feel that it is a setup to assign guys from different sets to work together for a week and not expect them to develop a strong friendship.

It would be called a "particular friendship," which I think is rooted in homophobia. When men are forbidden to be with each other for simple social exchanges, it can be perceived as a challenge to see how much they can get away with.

This is human nature expressing itself; however, anyone caught fraternizing is subject to severe penance or even expulsion.Contrary to Abbot Richard's fear, it is not a gay relationship, and try as he may, he cannot deter the ones that might develop into something more. It is just a hunger for a friend, for some personal connection. But it is forbidden, like the proverbial "forbidden fruit."

It is the two of us digging potatoes, providing plenty of time to get to know each other. No one will report us. Justin tells me a little about himself. He'd been cast out of his family because they caught him with another man alone in a bedroom and dumped him in this monastery.

I, of course, don't have anything to say about why I'm here. It must appear strange to Justin when I present myself as a mystery man.

CHAPTER 28

Not Another Zachary Situation

WHEN I spot Justin, I ease my way down the corridor. I'm just about to wave when Prior Richard comes walking with intent, rosary clicking in staccato cadence.

My throat tightening, I tiptoe into the shadows.

"Brother Justin, on your knees."

I am horrified.

"See me after Vespers," Prior Richard said.

I want to follow Justin when he leaves the chapel and darts toward Prior Richard's area, but I think better of it.

I shorten my time out at work and get myself back inside, hoping that I haven't missed Justin's trip back from Prior Richard's, wondering and worrying about what penance he has received.

It can be assumed that if you are called to the Prior's office, you walk out or drag yourself out with a hunched back and head, carrying a heavy penance.

I've made it in time; he's walking toward me with his head down. When he sees me, he has a pained look on his face. As I make my approach, he puts his arms and hands up, signaling me to refrain from advancing one step farther.

I'm confused. As I ask him how things went for him, he puts the trembling pointer finger of his right hand up to his lips while pressing his left hand toward the floor.

His beautiful blue eyes are swimming in tears.

I can't begin to imagine what had occurred in that hellhole of an office. I dread that thought that Prior Richard could have struck him with his holy hand or stick, as it has been rumored of him in some cases.

Something is terribly wrong. I open my mouth to speak, but I close it. I don't know what to say. He's acting so private. I figure I can get him to talk about it the next time we are working together, which will probably be tomorrow.

I've enjoyed our free time together. It's made our work fun. Eeek, I know we aren't supposed to have fun. And we're not supposed to be friends.

"No pf's, no pf's." Doesn't Prior Richard know that it continuously storms through our heads?Justin takes a tenuous step closer to me to drop the bomb, blowing up my heart.

He let out a sharp breath and said, "I can't talk to you anymore; we can't be seen together ever again, and I won't be working with you ever again; you are not to approach me ever again."

I am unable to respond, even if I had something to say. "Whys" are senseless. It is final. The one person I feel some kind of special connection with is shutting us out of my life. With a sinking feeling in my stomach, I nod in acknowledgment, turn, and walk far away from my lifeline as my world spins out of control.

I worry about Justin. I check every night to see if he is in bed. No one can forbid me from caring for and about him from afar, albeit with a dark sense of dread.

I am not certain if I am dreaming or seeing something real. Through my bleary, sleepy eyes, I'm seeing a specter-like figure that appears to be Justin walking toward the door. When I realize I'm not dreaming, I squint through the wavering flame of lantern light as it casts ghostly shadows on the lumpy walls.

Tears distort my vision further. I place the back of my hand against my eyes to restrain the flood of silent, screaming inner pain, etching lines down my face.

When I lower my quavering hands, no one is there. The doorway is empty. The truth will reveal itself tomorrow. Before I have time to process what I am seeing, I fall back to sleep.

I awake in a stupor, as if from a nightmare. It will soon be time to rise for the 3 a.m. Lauds. When I get to the chapel, I have no chance to check Justin's bench to see if he is there. It is way too dark in here. We are expected to chant by rote. We go back to our beds to rest a little more before returning for Prime at 6 a.m., where we receive instructions for the day and head out to work for a while.

Francis is working with me to harvest garlic, onions, and carrots. It is back-breaking work. But soon we will be back lying on the floor for Terce and seated on our uncomfortable benches for High Mass.

Our set is expected to rush out of the chapel and get on our knees to ask for prayers. There are no knee pads either. You just position your knees so each one is on a fairly flat stone. You can hear, "Please, brother, have the charity to pray for me," patterned like a song sung in a campfire round as each of us requests prayers of the brother swishing by us.

Swinging around the non-existent clock at noon for Sext, we finally get to sit down for the midday meal. This is when I get to see if Justin is still here. As I take my place on my bench at the table, we have a repeat of the Zachary scenario—no sign that a Brother Justin ever existed. Those brothers who used to flank him at the table are now side-by-side.

We are expected to just go on as if there never was such a person here.

The universe is held together by balance. Everything exists in a state of equilibrium: then and now, comfort and discomfort, friends and strangers, play and work, the known and unknown, togetherness and isolation.

I feel as if my universe has been shaken like pairs of dice landing on discomfort, strangers, work, unknown, and isolation. I think I'm due a session with Abraham.

I am driven to make real a scheme I've been toying with in my mind. I have enough time to look out front. Maybe Cordelia is out there looking for me. Maybe she's been there all along.

I rush toward the back door. I don't care if anyone sees me; I am out of here. I've had it. For some reason, I've never checked out front. I slide with my body against the stones under the tall windows to get back to where this all began. Back to the 21st century…

Cordelia, wait for me; I'm coming.

CHAPTER 29

••••••••••••••••••

A Storm is Brewing

NOBODY CARES. The stars don't even care. The gray clouds suit my mood. Francis is back outside working with me. I suggest that Abraham work close by so I can vent to him. I know I can trust Francis; we've become good buddies.

There are just the carrots left to pull, so Abraham and I can move on to gathering ferns, which are good for soups and stews.

Francis said, "I'm happy to work alone today; the sooner I get finished here, the sooner I can get to my chickens; those girls have been laying extra eggs, which means the cook will have more watery scrambled eggs to go around."

How metaphorical: mud is sucking my feet down. I'm stopping every few yards to kick my boots free of the allegedly drained swamp, which is more like a bog. As I remove a dry clot of mud-like cakes of dried cow flops, the last of the colors swirl off the nearly leafless branches. A vast swampland of muck surrounded us. The wind is kicking up, causing bushes and tree limbs to writhe and shake. A storm is brewing. I hope this isn't another foreshadowing. All the others I have tuned into were pretty accurate. Look where I am. I can't help but notice the blood-tinged sunset. What is going on in this world of mine? Why am I getting this creepy inner dowser experience?

The low carpet of sky is growing progressively darker and angrier. There is evidence of a gathering storm. Is it just nature, or is it more than that?

Rain is beginning to lash the muck. Ferns do love wetlands; otherwise, they turn brown quickly. I'm sure this is why Abbot Richard wants them harvested by tonight.I have to admit that in the 21st century, I do not care for fiddlehead ferns, and I guess maybe this is one of the reasons why. I can't imagine what fern tastes like after having delicious kale and rhubarb Swiss chard.

Here I am with the coveted opportunity to be heard by Abraham. I can't tell him much, though. I can't reveal to him how I flipped out, desperate to get out of here, escaping the 16th century and that I snuck outside through the back door where we are allowed to access our designated work section. But I went farther, into forbidden areas.

The front is where the offices are and where Prior Richard looms. I've been too afraid to go out front. We're not even allowed anywhere outside of our designated working area. I needed to sneak around to the front. That is where we were standing, waiting for the shuttle to take us to the Tor.

I can't admit I believed I could actually find my way back to the 21st century by just running to the front of the building. I can't talk to Abraham about that.

I can't tell him how sure I was that others from the harp therapy course would still be there waiting for me and if they hadn't left yet.

When I made my way to the other side of the building and out to the front, my friends were not there. The road was sparkling with water.

Between the shimmering of diamond-like drops and my swirly tears, all I could see were the soldiers with swords on muted, clopping horses, escorting wagons on sloshing wheels.

There was some medieval-dressed stranger knocking on the monastery's front door, probably bringing money to ensure and enforce our penitence.

I returned to the rear entrance, discreetly deserted, and resigned my efforts to get back to the 21st century. I will practice Eckhart Tolle's advice and stop resisting this Twilight Zone reality.

To avoid this sense of failure trapped and held hostage by the past, my obsessive thoughts returned. Had any other of my friends been portaled from out front?

As we stood waiting, in the 21st century, for the shuttle to take us to the top of the Tor, there was only the shell of this building remaining, with a broad wall supporting a large printed board recording the history of this place.

A man tried to pass by me, causing me to step into darkness. The darkness was lit by 16th-century lanterns. And here I am to stay.I can't help but wonder if any others are here experiencing what I'm going through and if they're working as hard as me to figure out who is who in the 16th century. I will never know, and they will never know about my trauma. What a place to be.

While at the evening meal, I happened to catch a shocking sight. It is the condition of one of the senior monks' hands. Actually, it is his fingers, or more precisely, his fingertips. They are black. I am quite certain it isn't as a result of the penance of having them struck with a stick.I promise myself I'm going to keep an eye on him and make sure he doesn't get sick. Day after day, I'm relieved to see him at his place at the table. I wonder how long it will take before it has a fatal impact on him.

Rivulets begin to bead on my forehead. It can't be.

It can't be. He's missing; Brother Harold, the black-ink finger-tipped monk, is sick, maybe even dying. It's just like in the movie "The Name of the Rose." What a horribly dark movie, and it's happening here.

CHAPTER 30

Reflecting Positivity

I HAVEN'T seen any other poisoned fingertips. Hopefully, it's only him. I don't know what I will say if I am ordered under the Vow of Obedience to copy a book with a quill dipped in poisoned ink.

I don't want to touch poisoned ink. I don't want to die. I don't want this to be the way I move from one lifetime to the next.

Just as I am mentally and irrationally lining up a major job for James, who works with the sick, there is a disruption at the end of the table. A few monks stand to make room, allowing another monk to shuffle to his place on the bench.

I can't see who it is at first, then my sweating face changes to beet red, accompanied by a sickening sinking sensation. I have fabricated all of this drama in my starving imagination.

The monk just situating himself at the table is Harold, the main character in my illusionary movie. He paralleled so well the setting and plot of the horrible movie, "The Name of the Rose."

The plot of the movie I was weaving into my already dramatic life was a story about monks with black ink on their fingertips. It turned out there was someone trying to kill the monks. The assailant had poisoned the ink they unknowingly dipped their quill tip into.

Whenever they touched the page they were writing on, getting ink on their fingertips, poison was slowly seeping into their bloodstream.

Slowly, the monks were being wiped out. As one copier of books mysteriously died, another took his place, to soon meet the holy coffin and the afterworld.

My 16th-century lifetime is so bizarre that attempts on our lives could be happening in this monastery. I swear, we have so much money coming in each day that it would not be difficult for someone to justify taking us all out, and I don't mean for a date.

The harvesting is complete. When we were hacking long sheaves of grain in a large group, even though we were to refrain from conversation, I found it an opportunity to hear a phrase from brother Stephen—my dear Cordelia. It fed my starving heart.

Francis is busy getting things ready for his girls to be warm without burning the place up. He wants them to be able to lay eggs safely. He is gathering the last of the hay for them, left from our pitchforked piles for the Jersey girls.

Francis is thrilled, and talking to his flowers and the egg-laying girls has been extremely productive. Everyone smiles when they see the occasional gruel-like serving of scrambled eggs. It is a nice change from the real gruel.

As the days grow drearier, the beautiful myriad of flowers he has heartfeltly tended brighten the soul in the flickering lantern light. Joseph labors daily in the near darkness, designing the gift of blossoms from Francis.

Together, they have raised my. . . hopefully. . . our. . . spirits to know they care for each of us. It is vital in this harsh, cold, heartless environment to know we are valued, even if it is shown by flowers and how they are displayed. Thank you, Francis. Thank you, Joseph.

I do a lot of video chats with several friends who are here, er, I mean in the 21st century. I have begun to piece together who Joseph and Francis are.

Mary Jo's labors for every holiday produce lovely decoration.

The entire interior of her home looks like a theme museum or something from a Home and Garden magazine. Hers is homier, and another friend, Jill, would prefer more to be featured in the garden section.Jill spends many of her peaceful moments taking pride in her fiery blooming flowers on her back deck and throughout her backyard. They are a breath of fresh air to behold.

I think it is quite clear that Joseph will be reborn into the 20th century as Mary Jo, my friend from Pennsylvania, whom I will meet in a dowsing group. We will become very close, sharing our understanding of energies and ley lines. She is also, like Cordelia, an inner dowser.Francis is Jill, with whom I will work from time to time over the years. We found a comforting commonality with our ADD (attention deficit disorder). We both tend to see "shiny objects" when attempting to get something done or stay focused on a task. We laugh a lot about our behaviors. She has the gift of being able to laugh at herself.

Poor Cordelia; she's always needing to tap me on the shoulder to draw my attention back to focus. She caught me when I was lost in thought about meeting with other participants and their companions in waiting at the harp therapy course.

That was the way she gently woke me, hand on shoulder, then tap, tap. I miss someone putting their hand on my shoulder and tapping. There is no touching or body contact here.

It is a wonder the :failure to thrive" we see in babies who are never held doesn't occur here. Maybe it does; we will never know. This is why the PF rule is often broken.

I've seen several couples hugging and kissing, especially when outside among the ferns or high-growing grains. I couldn't see who they were, except I think one was Abraham and someone else. The others were from another set—no one I know.

CHAPTER 31

Concerned Direction

IT SEEMS we should still be back in the fall, when we could freely be outside. Somehow, we have jettisoned into winter. How could that be?

It was summer when I was standing out front with the others from the harp therapy group, waiting for the shuttle to take us up to the Tor. I was swelteringly warm standing in line, reading the sign about this place.

Oh, how I wish I had time to read the entire history of this Glastonbury Monastery. I've heard whispers; it's turning cold, with snow falling frequently.I have to go out to milk the cows and see my girl Alfalfa, who lets me warm my hands against her warm udder. I have to do that before I milk her because it is her udder that holds the warm milk. Any warmth goes with the milk into the wooden bucket.I betcha; many a monk has dunked his freezing, numb hands into that soothing warmth. It's time to bite the bullet and put my big girl, er, big boy pants on to brave the chill. I better hurry.

We each have scheduled tasks. Mine is to milk the three cows. I am relieved that my first task is something I already have knowledge of, as I used to help milk the cows at my grandparents', where, as I have mentioned, we spent a portion of our summers.As I shoulder into my light-weight dark cape, Brother James catches me in mid-motion on my way out the back door, leading to my girls, who are definitely lowing by now, waiting for my attention.

James kindly advises me, "It is bitterly cold out there, and there's deep snow on the ground; please, wear your woolen mittens and boots with your Coptic socks and your woolen cowl."

After dressing as directed, I am deeply affected by the caring way he instructed me. Unlike so many incidences of what is called blind obedience, such as watering a dead stick, he explained why I needed to bundle up and used the word "please."

Blind obedience is defined as obeying an authority figure without thought. This is done regardless of the consequences of the actions that are being carried out. They also obey, whether or not the task they are asked to carry out makes any sense.

I know it's winter, and I know how cold it is when the scent of wood-fire smoke stings my already nearly closed nostrils. The cold is cracking and splintering the air as I jostle through the snow to get to my jerseys. I am doubly grateful to James for alerting me to these conditions.

I reluctantly remove my nicely knitted, yummy mittens, gifted to us by John. I was going to say, "Gifted to me," but nothing is mine; it is ours, given to us.

These community mittens could easily be taken from me for someone else if the brother's need presented itself to be more vital than mine, although I trust that my current need will win out.

James so lovingly reminded me to put them on for the first part of my venture. However, as wonderful as these mittens may be, they are no good for when I'm actually milking the cows. My fingers sting from the biting cold. I knot, release, and knot them again, trying to get feeling back into my appendages.

My excruciating dilemma reminds me of the man in Jack London's short story, "To Build a Fire." I know it will be futile, but still, I rap my lifeless hands against my legs.

"Nothing; just hurry and get yourself back inside." I'm muttering aloud to myself. It's a good thing no one's here. I can't tell, except by sight, if I have a sufficient grasp on the wooden pail.

To try to clutch it by its rope could be disastrous. I hugged it; it was the first time I had hugged anything or anyone in what seemed like an eternity. If I ever get back to the 21st century, I will hug everyone, holding on as if I'm never going to let them go again.

In the midst of my painful trauma, there it is, all frosted over, staring at me through the smokey fog. There is a legend that the Devil asked Dunstan, now St. Dunstan, who used to be Brother Dunstan, to re-shoe the Devil's horse. Instead, Dunstan nailed a horseshoe to the Devil's hoof. It was painful for the Devil, but Dunstan told him it would be taken off if he promised to never enter a place where a horseshoe hangs over a door. As the story goes, the Devil has kept his promise to this day.

James meets me under the doorway with the horseshoe hung upon it to direct me to the warming fire. He told me what to do next.

In a nearly inaudible whisper, he said, "Go into the kitchen to warm your hands; it will sting and ache terribly, so put them close to the fire, but not too close."

"Should I rub my hands together?" That's what I'd seen as a child on Western TV shows.

My new dear friend cautioned me in gestures and in hushed words. "No, don't rub them; just turn your wrists back and forth, and when your hands are warm, I have a couple pairs of thick gloves with warm cotton on the inside and outside."

I will not ask how he squandered or gained the privilege of having healing glove-like mittens; just be grateful. They are probably more like our strange socks, called Coptic socks.

My hands don't even feel like they belong to me. Wool double socks don't sound so bad if they help them get better. With the twisted messages going to my brain, I'm sure this must be someone else's pain from someone else's hands I'm bearing.

CHAPTER 32

Cacophony Erupts

THE FACT that James is the one giving attention to my torment is healing in itself. Though fireplaces are often depicted as locations that are dreamy and romantic, this fireplace was over 5 feet tall and 5 feet long. It could warm up the entire first level of a building.

As I squat here in the warmest corner of the kitchen, watching flames lick around the firewood, I am sweating for two reasons. One is obvious; the other is that I have the scorching realization that I am going to be here indefinitely.

As I am wont to do, I quickly snuff that burning thought out, turning to my pastime of figuring out who is who in the 16th century. I am sure James is Evelyn, who will be reincarnated to become a nurse in the 21st century.

Evelyn told me some interesting stuff to imagine with joy: "It's the 20th century, and the Ball family welcomes their first child. They named her Evanjalene Margaret Ball. She is born into money, political influence, and good breeding.

She is born two weeks late, and her mom is placed on bed rest in the hospital. When it was suggested that she might stay longer, her mother said, "No, I feel completely comfortable at home, and I want my own bed."

Evelyn radiated a big, beautiful smile when she was finished with the lovely vignette. It was then that I knew how my dear friend had come to have her strong sense of determination. I miss her smile. Although, looking into James' eyes, I can see a beautiful soul shining through.

Spirits are renewed as I jaunt toward our resting room. My reflection is disrupted, with great cacophony erupting, near Brother Richard's office, or, as I refer to it, his haunt.

I jostle my head this way and that. There are too many things blocking my clear vision. One of the robes moves aside for me to peer through those circling the poor brother, whomever he is.

It's Abraham on his knees with a feral gaze. Something is seriously amiss. I hope he hasn't been found out for his PF behavior or his kind counseling of everyone in our set.

The yelling escalates as more higher-ups gather. I cannot understand anything any one of them is barking about or comprehend what is going on. Each angry word slices across the undulating walls of the cold, unfeeling stones.

There are several brothers or abbots in black robes whom I have never seen before. Then, I spy something that completely befuddles me. This issue must be something out of the ordinary. The one creating the most vibrations, holding a thin stick in his shaking hand, has to steady his scarlet hat. Being enrobed in full scarlet attire indicates to me that he is a Cardinal, an emissary to the Pope. Surely, no such behavior as Abraham has engaged in could possibly bring on such a frisson of frenzy.

I hope he uses the stick only as a cane and for no other purpose. I cannot see Abraham anymore. He has been edged behind the doorway. As the scolding voices endure, I worry Abraham won't. The din is silenced, so I assume Abraham is getting his chance to explain himself and defend himself. I am sending a shield of protection and healing on all levels, accompanied by clarity, patience, and compassion, to the inquisitionist. It feels like the grand inquest is being reenacted, or maybe it hasn't happened yet in our history, here in the 15th century.

If the Inquisition has already occurred, then the Catholic Church is already well practiced in its techniques; this is beginning to feel like it.

That certainly was a time of sheer horror. As a young adult in the 19th century, I used to repeatedly play the soundtrack for "Man of La Mancha" on my cassette player. My favorite was "Dulcinea," which is such a sweet song.Only recently have I discovered that the entire musical is based on someone coping during the Inquisition. It gives me nightmares to think of it. Don Quixote wasn't crazy after all, tilting at windmills. He lived in insane times and found a harmless way to remain sane.I fear to imagine how Abraham will fare. Although, as of yet, I don't have any idea what his crime is or if I ever will.

I wonder where Joseph is during all of this imminent threat of violence and if he is any closer to knowing what is going on. Or would Sylvester have a better perspective?

While everyone in charge is preoccupied, I will break silence and every other rule to see if I can figure anything out about this volatile situation and what could possibly be its catalyst.

I suspect we will see another Zachary situation. I don't know; have there been more? I've lost track. Dear Abraham will no longer be at prayer, and his place at the table will be nonexistent.

My heart is a kaleidoscope of emotions. The shapes reflected are all sharp, stabbing, cutting to the quick, and maiming to the marrow.

A couple of days have passed since, as predicted, the wonderful companion for the group, Abraham, vanished. Everyone will have to solve their own dilemmas. There will no longer be a kind, nonjudgmental, ever-available ear for them.It's ironic how earlier I was praising Abraham in my mind and wondering what people would ever do if he were no longer here. He was such a wonderful help to so many troubled brothers. I'm not sure how things will smooth out between them and some of the brothers from other sets.

I can sense a definite change in morale. The unknown, like a god, has the most power to kill the spirit. I used to notice that when the substance abuse patients were waiting for an opening in their hoped-for recovery institution, the longer they waited for word, the thinner their confidence and hope grew. I fear to see that here.

CHAPTER 33

Deception

HERE I am, Madeline of the 21st century, sitting in the 16th century as Brother Samuel, questioning my sanity. What is happening to me and to others? And now one of the heroes, Abraham, of this bizarre story of our lives, is gone.

With no answers or explanation, the more days that pass without Brother Abraham to give counsel, the wearier the brothers grow. I do my best to let them know I'm here for them, but they don't know me, nor do they easily trust me.

Deception is a cruel player in the game of life. It masquerades as something it is not. It endears itself to us, and we reciprocate, playing into its cold clutches, aimed at our vulnerable hearts.

Our woundedness confuses us, plunging us into the throes of denial. We search for reasons, for an unobtainable logic, for a void in which to place the blame.

There is an important break in protocol when we do not assemble for the purpose of receiving our daily tasks. Instead, we are told by Abbot Richard to reassemble in one hour and to follow the directives of yesterday in the meantime.

There are whispered murmurs, indicating a raised level of tension and stress, as we depart, attending to our designated areas. Will my question, "What is going on?" ever be answered?

When we reconvene, goose bumps cover my arms, and the hairs on the back of my neck surely stand up.In front of us, on guest benches, are the same men I had seen forming a vigilante mob. They circle Abraham near Abbot Richard's office.

What are they doing here? Haven't we had enough of this "rubbing salt into our fresh wounds"? We haven't even had time to begin to mend or grieve. Little did I know we were about to receive further slashes that would make us feel as if we'd been run through with a dull, double-edged sword.

The rigid silence was broken by Brother Richard. "He is an imposter and a horrible heretic." We, of course, know to whom he is referring and will resistantly and defensively listen to every word.

Abbot Richard winced, pounding his thigh, as he continued, "We should have known something was askew; Abraham is a Jewish name. He has been expelled from this monastery and will be excommunicated. The irony is that this is not Abraham's first time being expelled from a monastery.

"He once was a member of a Russian monastery as a rabbi. For some reason, he was expelled from there. Instead, he and a rogue group of the Coptic religion gathered additional Jews for their cause."

As Abbot Richard pauses, I take time to mentally file this information. Coptic? Huh? That's the same name as our strange knitted socks. I'll have to look up the origins if I ever get back to the 21st century.

The disgusted Abbot continued on with his rant.

"Abraham must have tired of that game and came to our door making false claims; he'd been abandoned by his Christian parents and sent to our monastery.

"We express horror to think he partook of the sacrament of Holy Communion and wasn't even a member of the Catholic faith.

"There have been a growing number of heresies. That demands increased efforts to defend the Catholic faith. Usually, we do not comment on brothers who choose to leave, but this is our way of fighting heresies.

"With a reputation like this, our entire monastery holds the risk of becoming excommunicated. What would we do? No communion, no sacraments, not even confession? What would be our reason for existing? We might as well disband our whole group.

"Continue to follow the routine of tasks you have begun for the day. I remind you to be diligent in praying your rosary. Your mind should be on that rather than this matter.

"There should be no more discussion of this affair; it is being addressed and dealt with."

That's it, Abbot Richard, and holy higher-ups, just sweep this whole affair under the proverbial carpet with your straw broom. I guess the Catholic Church doesn't look at excommunication as a punishment per se, whatever that expression means. It's like giving said heretic a "time out."

Is Abbot Richard intimating we'd all be considered heretics? We, as baptized members of the Roman Catholic Church, would look like we were refusing to acknowledge or accept the teachings of that church.

It occurs to me that there is an irony here. Since Abraham was never a baptized Roman Catholic, it is empty words to say he is to be excommunicated. He won't care if he can never receive Holy Communion or other sacraments.

I'm wondering what corner Abraham is curled up in and what his next trick will be. I don't know whether to be angry at him, hurt by his façade, or spend my time remembering the good he did.

It reminds me of the story we've told from time to time about the mean man who was evicted and expelled from his town.

He went to live a couple of towns away and wore a mask of kindness, so he would not be recognized. Someone from his former town recognized him by the leather boat shoes he traditionally wore. The informer plotted to expose the masked imposter at a concert that night. When he rushed up to the microphone to tell the whole town there was an extremely mean and deceptive person in their midst, the volume of murmuring increased as the curious scanned the crowd.

At last, they all demanded to know the name of the accused. In response to their demand to know the man's identity, the accuser pointed at the man, whom they knew to be one of the kindest citizens in their town.

They yelled, "We do not believe you; you are mad."

The man with the microphone retaliated, "He is a very mean man and has been pretending to be kind by wearing a mask that only looks like a kind façade."

Mob psychology was displaying itself as he demanded action, saying, "Tear his mask from his face, and you will see I know from whence I speak; under that mask lives a mean, mean man."

Five individuals stormed toward the person of interest, dragging him to the grandstand in full sight of those gathered. Though he offered no resistance, he was treated with the rough restraint that is due a criminal.

There were great gasps from men, women, and even children when the mask of the town resident who had been accused of deception was ripped from his face.

Beneath the mask was the face of a kind man. He had pretended so hard for so long to be a gentle person; he had become one.

Maybe that is the case with Abraham. He helped so many of us. His kindness and self-giving couldn't all be for pretense, not with us, his brothers. Was nothing of what he said and did sincere? I catch bemused expressions on my brothers' faces. I wish I could help them sort this out.

Abraham would be able to help. He could take each of us aside, as he did so many times, working with us to sort out bewildering situations in our interactions with others, especially regarding run-ins with Prior Richard. If given a chance, Abraham would be able to explain himself. Surely there must be some logic behind his actions.

CHAPTER 34

The Mask

I SIGH deeply. That is what happens, isn't it? When we have a solid belief about something or someone and it is shattered, we begin to feel like broken pottery. We pick up the shards, attempting to glue the jigsaw puzzle of our lives back together.

For some, it holds, but for the fragile, the recovery is never firm. I send healing on all levels for those who need it and will receive it, including Abraham.

I need to quiet the buzzing that is chain sawing my brain causing an excruciating ache and head for the chapel.

Amidst the mélange of acrid body odor. the lovely fragrances of the flowers that Francis tenderly grew and Joseph caringly placed, and the sweet incense, I meditate, trying to soothe my savage soul.

What is that? I hear something that indicates to me that I've found heaven. This is not the kind of thing religious people speak of, nor does it have a sexual connotation, nor is it a dietary reference. This is different. Its origin is something comfortingly familiar.

One favorable thing Benedict promoted in our way of life was for anyone who had a skill or talent to foster it for the sake of the community.

My talent is teaching the brothers how to milk our three Jersey-bred cows. Some of the brothers had a sweet talent that they must have continued from one lifetime to another.

Cheating and peeking through my eyelid slits, I verify the information my auditory senses are feeding me. At first, I just see fingers plucking strings, not of steel but of what I know is called thin catgut. I don't really know all the gross details. I guess they made it from something from animals.

The angelic pluckers each hold a thin flat box with a good-sized hole cut in it, not as pretty as in the 21st century.

Chords are being played on harps, not by just one brother but by five. I memorize who they are so I can study them later. There is dear, sweet Cordelia as Stephen and Evelyn as James. Which one is Caren or Karin? Is that Mary Jo and Cyndy playing too? I cannot see their hooded faces, but I know they are there.

I am reminded of how, in the 21st century, these friends are taking lessons to be harp therapists. When certified, they will go into hospitals, homes, and nursing homes to play a specific set of chords to heal the sick and suffering.

We were, before this jolt of changing centuries, accompanying them as companions while they took their harp lessons. We were excited to be invited into the instruction area and have the opportunity to observe a fascinating demonstration of the effects of certain chords. We learned that when several notes are plucked at the same time, creating a chord, they have a different emotional, physical, or spiritual impact upon us.

It matters not to me what chords they play on the 16th-century harps. Every stroke of the string is healing. I no longer feel as isolated. I find myself studying their eyes, "the windows to the soul."

It reminds me of a poem from high school about how someone recognized a person familiar to them from the Titanic by looking into their eyes, under the brim of a hat, and seeing waves crashing, people screaming, and water overtaking their last gasps for air.

This feels peculiar. Unless we've been in other past lives together, and we probably have, I am, in the 16th century, looking to the future with memories of experiences with these friends not yet forged.

CHAPTER 35

· · · · · · · · · · · · · · · · · ·

Ripped Robes

I KNOW what I have to do. I don't know why I haven't thought about confirming my gut feelings before. I've consistently searched out evidence. I guess I've been caught up in too many incidents of drama in this medieval monastery. I will use the long, heavy string of beads on my rosary to dowse. The crucifix at the end will give proper weight to complete the pendulum. A pendulum is anything that swings, and this will do just right.

I will also send a peaceful healing energy message to these, my 16th-century friends. I will dowse about this mystery of identity and location. I will find out to what degree I am accurate in identifying my 21st-century friends in this, the 16th century.

Settled into a quiet place during one of our stingy rest periods, I ready myself to dowse. As planned, I want to verify the situation as it is unfolding regarding who is who in this monastery. However, I find myself being drawn to dowse about something more compelling.

There are two monks who always sit next to Abbot Richard at the head of the table. Last evening, one of them, named Brother Roger, was missing. I was quite sure this was not a Zachary situation, reminiscent of a brother named Zachary who must have done something taboo. He simply disappeared and was never spoken of again.

Unlike Zachary, Brother Roger's seat at the table remains empty. I detect clues that something else is afoot. As many know, I am easily distracted, finding it difficult to focus. However, my big browns could not unfasten from the spectacle of Brother Richard's fidgeting upon his bench. In an attempt to distract him from whatever is troubling him, he grants a free day with the magic Latin phrase "Benedicamus Domino."

We answer uninformed and mindlessly, "Deo Gratias", followed by applauding and hoopla-ing. We will be able to talk the entire day without incurring a penance.

Though many are preoccupied with the sudden, surprising free day, I'm fixated on studying Brother Richard's intense exchange with his buddy, Brother John.

Both appear stiff and uncomfortable, glancing around the room, frequently checking over their shoulders. What are they anticipating or fearing will happen?

That's what I want to dowse about, but I don't know where to begin. If or when Brother Roger returns, maybe Abbot Richard will relax. For now, he keeps rubbing his forehead as if he has one splitting migraine.

He taps his fingers, then raps his knuckles on the table as he routinely swivels his head with darting eyes. I've never seen this level of vulnerability in the Abbot. Hopefully, more will be revealed.

I move into our gathering room to see how everyone is doing. I take Sylvester, who does the financial bookkeeping, aside. He might have a more precise clue as to what sort of trouble is simmering.

When he finishes his explanation, I realize this place is a house of cards. A powerful storm will collapse it. He reveals how we have become a 'prayer factory' for the rich. We have become corrupt. What an ironic cautionary tale. It goes much deeper, or should I say, much higher.

Sylvester has learned the Holy Pope is a ruler with an army. This life is packed full of ironies. Both he and King Henry VIII want to close this monastery, actually all monasteries. I'd like to think of Henry the VIII fondly, as I remember Herman's Hermits' recording.

In high school, in the 20th century, I played it repeatedly on my 45, or to be more precise, my seven-inch 45 rpm vinyl record. Even though one of my favorite English rock groups sang it, I will probably never want to listen to it again, even though I'm sure I could find it online. Henry VIII has toppled from the pedestal I had him on.

The Pope, with whom I am unfamiliar, is down there in my mind's eye groveling on the ground too. Things are not looking good. I give a glimpse back toward Sylvester. As I am walking back toward our section, the giant wooden knocker is slammed several times against the front door. Among all the indelible memories within my brain, the countenance and disheveled condition of Brother Roger will remain ingrained. His robe was torn and muddied with stains of blood on his shredded sleeve. The most obvious source of the darkened brown splotches was his nose.

When he turned just right, I spotted a tear lined with reddish-brown near where his knee would land if thrown to the ground. With eyebrows knitted tight, I ponder what could have happened?

I am hoping there will be another break in protocol when Brother Richard substitutes in place of our described duties for the day, some sort of explanation, jagged as it may be, so we will be fairly and soundly apprised of what is coming next.

The drama escalates as Abbot Richard and Brother John catch Brother Roger just as he is about to collapse to the stone floor. Ow, that would hurt. There is some visceral pain, just imagining how that would rack his already battered body. With their support, he hobbles and ghosts into the Abbot's hostel or office.

CHAPTER 36

Sheep Without a
Shepherd

IN ADDITION to the shouting performance reminiscent of what we heard on the occasion of Abraham's confinement, there are the sounds of objects being thrown and bashed against stone walls.

Though Abraham, our favorite brother, was being called a lying heretic, there was never any indication that Abbot Richard had become this incensed.

I'm wondering if there is a connection between Brother Roger's battered state and the uneasiness I witnessed on our free day a few days ago. Is this what they were fearing? Do they have secret fears of something happening to them?

Days passed and all three brothers—Richard, John, and Roger—are among the missing. We are sheep without a shepherd, feeling like lost lambs. Out of habit, we manage to continue with the routines of the day.

Nothing is forgotten. It is weird how we still keep silence, with the reader hypnotically giving us the Rule of Benedict in monotone. No one says anything, but I am sure our anxiety level is escalating with each hour that the unknown looms over our heads, which, incidentally, I hope we can keep.

I detect a sigh of mixed emotions as each of the big three—Abbot Richard and Brother John, followed by Roger, whose left eye is betraying an ugly shiner—are all back at the head of our table. It feels like the spiral of life may be tilting closer to a balanced position.

With the usual required silence, we make an attempt to eat and to digest everything. The ferns in the soup seem to have been imbued with even greater bitterness. Ah well, more penance yields more money.

There will be a villager who will knock on the front door to donate money for our suffering. I wonder if there might be a bonus if they knew about Brother Roger's near inability to move due to some beating involving our money.

I notice the fingers of his left hand are wrapped in large leaves. I guess they haven't discovered gauze yet. My imagination is drawn to the movies and darts away as I review how the fingers are affected as a result of torture.

I assume Brother Roger left here willingly. Who did he meet up with? Was it someone who just wanted to get points for abducting and torturing a short-statured, roly-poly monk? I somehow don't think any townsfolk are responsible for his close scrape with death.

In anticipation, I watch and listen to the abbot, slurp by slurp and bite by bite, as his bowl empties. As the moment for our dismissal arrives, he breaks protocol and speaks.

He commends us for carrying on despite the absence of his guided instructions. In the same quivering voice, he instructed us to automatically resume our work assignments on schedule.

I am about to protest in my muttering mind at being left out in the dark when he speaks a second time. His whole being shakes as he stumbles through his instructions: "We h-have s-some very imp-portant matters to discuss. We'll forego Sect prayer, and the Kitchener has been informed that our noon meal may be delayed. It will be acceptable if

None prayer time is waived. Alright, be about your day's labors; bells will ring in a short while for Terce. I will see you here in the refectory after Mass."

Following Mass as instructed, we all file into the refectory or dining room. The tension in this room could be carved up with a fish-flaying knife as we wait for the abbot's arrival at his spot at the head of our refectory table. There is much shifting of postures on the benches. The brothers are doing their best to keep silence; however, if facial expressions made noise, there would be a high-pitched cacophony.

Here he comes. We all sit rigidly at attention. What is Abbot Richard going to tell us? Hopefully, we will find out what happened to Brother Roger, who is here too. He looks like he could use some serious painkillers, possibly opium, a popular painkiller in this era.

However, he doesn't look like he is managing his pain at all. Ooof. It occurs to me that he is suffering for others and will bring in several shiny shillings for the sovereign pontiff, or Pope.

It's papal property if he just takes charge. Who will win out? He, or the King? And will we, the unimportant monks, become involved? Or will it just concern those higher up? We shall find out. Everyone is settled in as Abbot Richard begins speaking.

Rubbing his forehead, he appears to be summoning the courage to continue. "I will not mince words. As you have observed, our dear Brother Roger, my attaché, was away for a while and returned in a ragged condition.

An audible sigh prefaces the abbot's resuming. "We received notice that we are to close this monastery. There are to be no more monasteries operating in England by word of King Henry the VIII with the putrid permission of the Pope." Wooden bowls rock as he pounds the table, punctuating the power of the word "putrid."

CHAPTER 37

The Knock on the
Door

THE ABBOT made a confession. " Had I known Brother Roger would be hemmed in by Henry's hateful henchmen, I would not have commissioned him to risk life and limb."

He mentioned that he knew it was his responsibility to care for the monks and keep them safe and housed. He did not want to send them out to be homeless.

I worry about where I would go, as I don't even know who I am as a non-monk in the 16th century. As I have said, I have no idea who I am, where I came from, or who I might be related to here in England. I'm glad Abbot Richard recognizes the dilemma many of us would be in. Although the Pope is in collaboration with the King, he reassured, "With no negotiating availed to us, we're just going to hold our ground. We know the Lord wants us to continue, so continue we shall in His Grace."

OMG. Now I'm rapidly recalling what that sign on the wall in front of this building said. This is not good. My friends and I have to get out of here. This information foretells a bleak future for us.

The abbot stands to make sure we are paying attention. With a commanding tone, he cautions us, "Be absolutely careful if your job for the day is porter—you may only open the door to familiar donors."

I don't think they had peek holes back in the 16th century; thus, the mandate should be 'do not, under any circumstances, open that door.' However, that would mean no moolah coming in.

Mark my word, money will find another way to undo us. Someone will knock saying they have a donation, and what they will be holding is not money but trouble and a bell to ring our death knell.

The tension eases as the tumultuous week comes to an end. We go about our monastic duties, some more interesting than others. Borrowing an idiom from the 21st century, the action plan for retaliating against the initial experience of being shaken up is put on the back burner. This may or may not be a positive thing. When minds rest, alertness sleeps.

During the winter, we are working on the frugal method of our lighting source, the rush. Not the sort of rush we speak about or attempt to achieve but a natural reed. We gathered them last summer to dry out. After stripping them of their skin, we soak them in animal fat to be used for lantern wicks.

The other need is for our personal candles. That procedure deals with the method of each of us dipping our individual candles into tallow. This requires something from two animals, one not so painful and the others more melted down animal fat. The tallow candle burns longer and brighter than the rush candle.

We find it tedious to stand in silence, speaking only to recite the rosary while continually dipping a wick of John's wool into tallow. John is our shepherd. After shearing the wool from his sheep, we made pieces into wicks.

I wondered how we would ever shear a sheep in the 16th century. Well, I found out. I'm saying sarcastically that the monastery must have spent a pretty penny to get those elegant shears. They weighed over a pound with some sort of spring blade, not a 'sling blade' spring blade. Uh huh.

But they did the job, and we gathered plenty for John to work with—to direct us on how to twist the wicks and comb the wool—and for him to prepare yarn for his creations, especially those Coptic socks. I want a dozen pairs of those to give out as Christmas presents. NOT.

Although they might be quite a crowd-pleaser, we could probably get them on eBay. I'll tell John and/or Cyndy they probably shouldn't plan on making a career out of that kind of knitting.

We are winding down from praying Terce at 9 a.m. and preparing for High Mass. Everyone freezes when what we call 'a policeman's knock' in the 21st century comes at our front door. Who would be knocking at the door on a cold November day?

Many excuse it as an ordinary donor headed for some destination. As the porter marches toward the door, I feel like reenacting the slow-mo scenes where someone, in an attempt to stop the walker, is running in slow motion and shouting in deep, drawn-out tones, 'nnooooooo,' but as in the movies, I would have been too late and ineffective.

One of the older monks robotically rises from his wooden prayer bench, but someone puts their hand on his hip to halt him. I take a breath of relief in and out as the blood pounds my temples and my throat grow dry.

The intruder knocks repeatedly, increasing the volume to an intimidating pulse. No donor would be this frantic and intent on giving away their hard-earned money. I fear the porter will weaken. He must remain steadfast in his refusal to open that door. Someone suggests he go consult the abbot before responding to the knocks, if that's what you can call them.

The knocking, which had turned into pounding, has suddenly changed into banging with muffled shouting as Abbot Richard appears around the corner. The banging has turned into a ramming sound. O-M-G. They are using some sort of battering ram. They'll be in here soon. Then what? That giant, thick wooden door is splintering.

We have nowhere to hide. We stand at the edge of the chapel, paralyzed. Abbott Richard directs us to turn inward toward the chapel to lay prostrate, possibly for the last time, upon this cold stone floor, which seems even colder and fills me with chills. I worry about my friends. What will happen to us? I know we will all make it to the 20th century sooner or later, so we will meet again.

CHAPTER 38

A Familiar Tapping

I WANT to put my hands over my ears and over my heart. Why do I feel like this is some sort of "goodbye"? I am very sad to give this report. I keep telling myself that you are having your last gaze into their beautiful soul for this lifetime. You know there will be others. You've been there. You will get there again.

The ramming and splintering have ceased. They are through. Ashen Abbot Richard, weakly and softly, with tears in his eyes, says, "You might as well rise and make ready for our impending doom and imminent death. I'm not sure how they will carry this out but they have won; they will have our monastery and all of our money."

At first, all I saw were black boots, until I shakily raised myself from the floor. Then all I saw was red.

A deep, gruff voice echoes throughout the halls. "We are the soldiers commissioned by His Majesty King Henry VIII to take control of this monastery, which will be no more.

"We command these three to come forward and kneel. John Thorne, Roger James, and Richard Whiting"

I'm sure their knees were shaking so badly that, after being helped forward, they almost tumbled. Then to have the strength to bend their knees to kneel. All three had to hold on to each other so as not to tip over once down on their knees.

Then they receive their sentences. The king is making a public example of them to deter any more resistance from any other monasteries. I saw this happen with first-time drug dealers in the 21st century. The judge wanted to make an example of them to deter any other one-time newbies.

"On this cold November day in 1539, you, Richard Whiting, will be declared the last abbot of Glastonbury. You are accused of and have been found guilty of taking 20,000 crowns [about £5,000] from the abbey funds."

As if the abbot stole money for himself. The money belonged to the monastery. He probably used it to purchase those expensive shears I talked about. Or maybe he used it for our care. What a concept!

I tune back into the bellowing voice of the lead soldier, still giving the sentence of our three leaders. "You will be carried up through the High Street on a horse-drawn hurdle and then up to the summit of the Tor."

I barely have time to put it together. Now I know why there was inner turmoil in the 21st century every time we saw the Tor on our trip here. This is why there were repulsive responses among us. I remember the descriptions of our impressions of the journey through the town of Glastonbury as we headed toward the Tor. It was all one big foreshadowing.

The head soldier is not finished ringing the death knell with his condemnations. "Richard Whiting, you will be hung on a gibbet with John Thorne and Roger James hanging on either side of you." That was just like the two thieves in the scene at Calvary.

Large, heavy grain sacks are placed over their heads, encompassing their bodies. As they are dragged out through the giant door splinters and down the primitive steps to some carriage, terror sets in. I am so filled with panic that I'm experiencing difficulty breathing. I'm fighting back tears. I avoid looking at my friends for fear I will break into loud sobs.

Early on here, it was as if I'd been transported into a world free of air pollution, noise pollution, hatred, and violence. Or so I believed. I thought I had my feet on the threshold of opposites.

I perceived this to be a placid, silent environment; I'm fully aware people kill each other where, or rather, when I'm from. I had not brushed up on the history of this era. Had I known I would be zooming into here and now, I would have been more prepared and more terrified.

The imposing soldier reappears all in red, a sword at his side. He is dressed in a peculiarly shaped black hat and white pants of all colors and is just a little more intimidating while holding a rifle. Are we going before a firing squad?

Soon comes my answer. "We will not hang you; we will only take your holy heads." We are herded into our gathering room. Benches are thrown into one corner, along with tables shoved aside and knocked over. The plan is to clear the floor space and have us kneel.

The executioner is making ready with his axe; a chopping block waits for each of us. Kneeling on the stained stones, I am next in line. He is so close; I can feel the heat of his bulging body. As he stands behind me, I wonder if the hand on my shoulder is to steady me from listing to the left.

That firm hand moves and begins tapping—that familiar tapping I had so longed for. My vision and hearing begin to blur. I can sense the hammering of my heart and the loud buzzing in my ears. Nothing else. I do not hear her.

"Madeline, Madeline." It was Cordelia, gently tapping and shaking my shoulder. "Madeline, hello."

....

CHAPTER 39

The Shuttle Eaves-Dropping

MY VISION cleared as I turned toward her. "Madeline, I've been trying to get your attention for about five minutes. I stepped away for a couple minutes to check on the shuttle's arrival time, and—you'll never believe where I ended up. It feels like a year. I'm so glad you are still here. Have you moved at all? Where did you go in your imagination? You and your ability to daydream."

That was far from daydreaming; it was a complete nightmare. Before Cordelia gets to finish what she was saying, all of the others who were waiting there rush over toward us. I blink as if coming back to my senses.

All of my friends are still alive and in one piece. I'm sure they think I'm acting strangely when I embrace them for long seconds. We'd been through the slaughter and are now on a new adventure in a safer time with better eating utensils.

Charred smears streaked up the stone walls, framing burned-out windows that once were our home of sorts. We stand there in a group, staring, holding hands, and embracing each other as if we're never going to let the others go again.

The shuttle arrives at that moment. I picture our portals pulsing behind us as we leave. I want to reunite our group. I said, "I promise, one and all, that we'll discuss this when we get out of this shuttle up at the base of the Tor." There is a hornet's nest buzz of conversation as we settle into the bus seats.

Tourists who were clueless about what had happened to us joined us. One woman says to another, "Oh, we've got to walk back down here to get some of that well water; it is said to have healing qualities." She taps on the bus window, indicating a sign reading The Chalice Well.

Her friend speaks my thoughts. "I don't know." There was a long pause. "I know we came here together to enjoy our tour, and I hope you won't be mad, but I think I'll pass on that."

Her friend comes back with a counteroffer. "But Sarah, don't you know it gives eternal youth to anyone who drinks it? Let me be near it. Quick!" She laughs, slapping her lap.

"No, thank you. I'm happy to be maturing at the rate I am. No need to slow that up. Besides, who would really want to live on a gerbil wheel forever? Not me, thank you."

Then she nailed it. "Besides, unless you are part Vampira, tell me why in the world anyone would be attracted to drinking blood-red water."

Sarah continues. "Is it just water, or does it belong to the murdered on this famous Tor? Back where we were waiting for this shuttle, I read that some soldiers did some serious damage to some monks years ago, up there on that Tor. Maybe his blood is mixed in with the water. Yuck, and you want to drink that?"

In spite of the background din, we are all listening to Sarah's friend, who it seems wild horses could not keep away from that well. "Why do you think it's called the Chalice Well?"

Sarah answers a bit defensively, "I don't know, Susie, why is it called the Chalice Well?"

I am reminded of the Michael line's dark, negative influence on people. The Michael ley line is an energy wave running below the surface of the earth that has a harsh, dark feeling to it and has been the driving force through our entire journey through England.

Are we witnessing Michael's effects on friendship?

Susie answers Sarah in a sing-songy tone. "It is called the Chalice Well because it is the blood of Jesus; now, you tell me you're going to refuse that?"

Fortunately, we've reached the entrance to the Tor, so we don't have to listen to any more. I think the answer is a look of disgust and blowing a raspberry, indicating the level of her frustration. They will have to settle that without our audience.

The bus driver has his assistant jump out to move the sawhorse that blocked us the first time we drove up here, telling us to turn around and wait for the shuttle. That seems like a year ago. Was it? Time is all messed up in my head. Maybe someone has a better explanation.

Everyone piles out, and we find a cushy spot under a shade tree to gather ourselves. We have so much to process. No one of us has anything to eat. I guess we expected that in such a tourist spot, there would be vendors. Instead, all they are offering is blood-red water from an ancient well.

I sense the memories fading fast. We've got to resolve things so we will never have these premonitory experiences again. We need to be healed of the horrors we've experienced so that that part of our past will be softened.

·····················

CHAPTER 40

Processing Begins

I COULDN'T wait to start talking and processing what happened to me first, then to the others. "I was standing there reading that big sign out front of that building. What was it? A museum? Karin and Caren, I saw you disappear into it; what was in there?"

Both looked at each other with concern and simultaneously said, "Darkness!"

"You too? As I was saying, I was standing in front of the sign describing the monastery's destruction and the circumstances surrounding it, which I never did get to read, instead I—"

I looked around at each friend who could have joined me for the remaining part of the sentence—you know how some people mouth the words with you as you speak? Well, there were many lips murmuring right along with my audibly spoken words. "I—stepped into darkness," I concluded.

There followed a chorus of "Us too... me too... the same thing happened here... there was just darkness... I ended up in some dark room that might have been a bedroom... I had no idea where I was or where everyone else was... I thought we'd been abducted and you guys were in some other room." This could have gone on forever. I decided to contain these reactions by having each of us tell our story.

"Whoa, let's each tell our individual story; I think that is important. I also think we will understand better why we had such dramatic and, in some cases, physical effects from seeing the Tor, pictures of it, or even the mention of it."

Then Cordelia reminded me of my adverse reaction to the plates in our cottage cupboard with the pictures of the very monastery where we were going to be transported.

Cordelia raised her eyebrows and shook her head in amazement. "No wonder I had to wash that plate; you were really having some kind of inner dowser premonition. I am supposed to be the great inner dowser, according to you; harrumph."

She turned, directing the information to the others. "We were having raisin biscuits and coffee for breakfast. When I pulled out the plates, Madeline freaked. I couldn't figure out what was going on with her."

Cordelia directed the next question to me. "Madeline, did you ever realize or mention to anyone that it was a specific picture on the plate that bothered you?"

I couldn't remember at this point; so much had happened. "I don't know. I just know it was as if the energy coming from my plate was too much for me to make contact with. It's like the powerful energy some of us sense at a yard sale.

"One of my dowsing friends, Mary, and I often experience weird energy at yard sales, garage sales, or tag sales. We look at each other with repulsed expressions as we drop an item we were holding because of its creepy vibes.

We always shake our hands, like I did as I quickly put that cottage plate down. This helps rid our beings of any negative energy."

Caren piped in, "Oh, I know what plates you're talking about. I made Karin get paper plates because I was not touching those plates. The large one may have been even worse than the little ones."

Mary Jo and Somara looked at each other and laughed, pointing fingers.

Evelyn summarized everyone's frustration: "I just had the greatest urge to smash all of them, but I did not want to get us kicked out of our place."

Cyndy laughed, "I thought I was going to have to yell, 'Evelyn, stand down; back away from those plates.'" Evelyn patted Cyndy's arm and gave her a hug with a big smile.

Everyone joined in the round of "Yes, those creepy plates… why would they put such pictures on them?… we had to buy paper plates too… it's a good thing we knew not to use those plates, someone would have to touch them to wash them." There was evidence of many shudders being thrown off, as if they were shaking off the proverbial dark dust of the past.

I looked at Cordelia fondly, gesturing toward her, and said, "She did wash one plate for me—we did a coin toss to see who would wash that one little plate we had used—she rigged the toss." Looking at her, I asked, "Didn't you?"

She shrugged, acting all innocent with a wicked grin on her face.

Bringing it all together for us, I added, "We might as well connect all of this to the Michael ley line. I think we've experienced the horrid events that have been tagged with the darkness of the Michael line. How could such dark energy run through our earth?"

Caren really was a lifelong student. "Do they travel through any specific spots in the world? I've heard that if there are certain power spots like Machu Picchu in Peru, there will be some ley lines present."

In answer to her question, I explained, "There are many ley lines running throughout the earth, creating havoc in some places while, in others, people claim to feel miracles happening, like in Sedona, Arizona, in our own country.

"The two basic ones running below the surface in England are the Michael and Mary lines. We experienced them at Stonehenge and the

Standing Stone Circle in Avebury, along with Silbury Hill, a very curious-looking pyramid. I read that the Mary and Michael lines crossed at that point. I guess it's like the yin-yang, where we stare at the balancing of things. Fortunately, the universe has provided the Mary ley line, the opposite of the Michael ley line.

"The energy of the Mary line, as we know, brings on a soft, fluffy feeling. We will become balanced, I promise you."

They were supposed to share their own stories of having been vortexed into the 16th century, but it has not really happened yet. There were too many other topics affecting them.

CHAPTER 41

The Dishwasher

WE FINALLY began sharing, but true to form, I was probably talking too much. But I promised them they could tell their stories. It will eventually happen, but first I need to begin.

"First of all, I will tell you who I was as a monk, though some of you may already have suspected it," I said, as everyone sat forward, wondering if they had guessed correctly. "I was Brother Samuel, and I was also worried we'd been abducted, and you and the others were alone in a dark room with just a bed in it.

"The walls of stone led me to think we were in some dank cellar, and I thought it odd that there were no light switches or wall plugs anywhere, as I felt around the room."

I saw plenty of nodding in the positive. "I got a penance the minute I hit the floor," I said, swinging my hand in a slicing action.

A couple of them giggled. Mary Jo said, "We saw Abbot Richard was preoccupied, so we quickly followed the only light bringing us to the chapel area."

"Yuh," Somara said, "we felt badly about using your dilemma as an opportunity to sneak in without getting caught for being late, but it was a matter of survival."

"But we pulled it off, and we were lying prostrate on those uncomfortable rocks when Prior came in," Cyndy said with a victorious grin.

Caren raised both hands with a grin from ear to ear. "He had no clue."

"Did you notice anything when you were lying there?" I asked, smirking and waiting for the answer while preparing the pronunciation of the important words for the joke I recited over and over in my head.

"When you were lying prostate, I mean prostrate, did you feel different?"

Cyndy was the first to start the laughing, creating a regular domino effect. "That's an eyebrow-raising question to answer." She quietly snickered. "I guess I noticed my lack of breasts and having something between my legs that wasn't there before. I wanted to stand and stare at it in disbelief, but knew that would have to wait."

Satisfied, I said, "I see I wasn't the only one who was surprised." We were all laughing by then.

Cyndy tended to be a thinker, so I was curious what her reaction would be. Now I knew. Bhaaa.

Somara said she now knew why her husband needed to adjust himself.

"All men have to do that, and now we know why," said Evelyn.

"I will never look sideways at my husband again," said Caren.

"To have that equipment their whole life, umph," said Mary Jo while making a face that we all echoed.

Karin confessed that she was wondering how long it would take to adjust to the new body.

Jill laughed with a surrendering gesture and blithely said, "No comment."

I guess we've discussed that nearly to the ground. But I still hadn't gotten to say my joke. "I got confused about the two words prostrate and prostate. Then to busy my mind or Samuel's mind, I played with the concepts, wondering if lying prostrate on those cold stones would bother someone's prostate."

"You do love wordplay, don't you, Madeline?" Cyndy knew me well. She'd seen me perform for our substance abuse patients many times.

"Okay, enough of the serious stuff," I said, and there was more laughter.

"I'm going to tell you who I think you were back then and see if you were wondering the same thing about each other.

"Cordelia, it was really hard to identify you; what did you do all day?"

My dear friend Cordelia, whom I had missed a lot, answered my many questions. "First, I will tell everyone here that I was Brother Stephen." There were nods of recognition from several as they snapped fingers, slapped their laps, or pointed with that expression of victory. "We knew it."

She continued answering my question: "Madeline, you're going to laugh. Remember how you needed me to wash that saucer with the triggering image of the monastery on it?"

"Yes, I certainly do. We've all discussed those plates ad nauseam. Right, everyone?" I looked around for confirmation—there were nods and groans. "So why are you bringing that up again, Cordelia?"

"Madeline, my dear friend, I know you've never liked wet wood, and I've watched how you've reacted with popsicle sticks or when there was a cooking spoon made of wood in your vicinity."

I was getting really frustrated. All I wanted to know, and I'm sure the others also did, was what she was doing in the 16th-century monastery since we never saw her there. She didn't need to keep prolonging the answer.

I tried to get my point across. "Another unpleasant subject. What in the world are you getting at? Why you said I'd laugh, I have no idea. So far, nothing is one bit funny."

"Madeline, let me finish; I'm answering your question. You wanted to know what I did all day. I have never minded wet wood. Good thing. My job or skill for the community was to… wash all those wooden plates, bowls, mugs, and eating utensils."

There were audible expressions of surprise, repulsion, and admiration. "Whaaat? You did that? Whoa. How could you? I guess she didn't have a choice. No, you certainly didn't have a choice."

It was difficult to separate the voices. We were all bewildered but relieved it wasn't us.

CHAPTER 42

Revelations

AS THE ladies lounged beneath a tree, it became obvious that this was a time for surprising revelations. Not everyone knew Karin had become a psychiatrist in the 20th century and was addressed in professional venues as Dr. Karin. However, in the 16th century, as Brother Abraham, she was misunderstood and misjudged.

Karin had been listening to Cordelia and wanted to add to the dishwasher's speculations about why she was not skeeved out by wet wood. Karin said, "Overexposure can curb aversion to unpleasantries."

Cordelia was impressed. "So, do you think that helped? I was on daily dish duty."

I could feel my teeth grating together and hoped no one heard them as I spoke. "That's why you were never out with us, harvesting or milking the cows. What was your name anyway, Cordelia the holy dishwasher?"

"Oh yes, I milked the cows but needed no instructions because we had cows when I was growing up; I was Brother Stephen."

"So next, Mary Jo, you were Brother Joseph, who was responsible for decorating the chapel. I knew that was you because of the elegant decorating that I've recently seen in your lovely home.

"And searching out who you were, Caren, I almost got myself another penance. That one would have been a humdinger. First of all, I was outside for no monastic reason, and second, I was sneaking into a mysterious building.

"That was the way I discovered Patrick was you. Every time we were outside, it was a relief. I'd scan the area, but there was never any sight of you until I finally got lucky and spotted you coming down the steps from some unknown building."

There were pleas from several. "Tell us what happened next."

I was excited to tell the story. It would go down as one of the happiest discoveries. I told them that I had been milking the cows and rushed the milk bucket to the kitchen bench, where I was supposed to leave it.

"I clandestinely hurried back outside with my obsessive thoughts about getting into that building. I knew if I could get into the back of the building, I wouldn't be discovered. There was only one complication. There was no door in the back," I said.

There were groans of concern from all. Caren, of course, was the most concerned. "What did you do? Had you gotten in trouble, I would feel horrible and somehow responsible."

I wanted to allay her fears. "I relaxed when it occurred to me that there was little chance of anyone seeing me because the windows were very high."

"Oh, that's right, there was no decorating them, bummer; I always regretted that." Mary Jo did like decorating.

I continued my account of how I got in through the front and about my discovery. "I was able to easily wedge the door open with a piece of wood. When I peeked into the building, I saw shelves filled with pottery.

"I finally knew where Patrick went every day and why we never saw him in the fields. And even better, I knew Patrick was Caren."

My discovery fascinated Jill. "Very cool." Then she addressed Caren. "That's right, you had all of those nice pottery pieces for each of us at the cottage. So, you were a potter in the 16th century, and now, in this lifetime. Very cool." She had a big smile on her face.

I had to share my silly wonderings. "You know, Caren, I've been thinking, what if we went to the museum of history and got to the 16th-century monastery section and saw your pottery? Wouldn't that give you goosebumps?"

Next, I turned toward Cyndy. "We would also see some of the Coptic socks you knitted. Wouldn't that be weirdly wonderful?"

Mary Jo jumped into the conversation. "We should do that while we're here in England. Oooh, let's do that. I wonder where we'd go. We should check it out."

After the laughter of agreement settled down, I directed my serious attention to Somara. "As a scourge of shame to the King and Pope exhibit, we would see the books you were forced to keep and protect, so that the museum-goers would then understand how the Catholic Church became so rich.

"On a more serious note, Somara, I will forever be indebted to you for saving me from a fate worse than death. Well, that idiom doesn't hold much water in light of the circumstances we were faced with in the 16th century, does it? Anyway, you, as Brother Sylvester, were aware that I was not doing well making my way to the abbot's office."

"You sure weren't; I knew I had to do something, so I pretended to drop stuff. That seemed to ground you. As bursar and working near Abbot Richard's office, I witnessed many brothers having to go kneel before him to get their penance or get released from it.

"They were as paralyzed as you, but I was too scared to do anything for them. When I saw it was you trembling and stuck, something said, 'Go for it boy'. I'm so glad I did."

"So am I." Turning to the others, I explained how Somara, as Stephen, came through for me. I had to go see Abbot Richard to get a review for release from my penance; I was terrified. If I made any mistake, I would get a new penance, and he could hand those 'babies' out like candy."

Mary Jo was concerned about what may have happened to Somara as Stephen for coming to the rescue of Madeline as Samuel. "Did you get in any trouble for interfering with the mood? I'm sure the abbot wanted to keep the air of fear strong."

Somara shrugged as she said, "All I paid for that saving grace for Samuel was to kneel with the book in front of everyone and drop it. I'm sure others here have similar stories that we need to hear.

You all know the feeling of the abbot coming to get you or sending for you. I found out later that I was to get penance for dropping the book at such a crucial time."

CHAPTER 43

Counting Sheep

SOMARA CONTINUED her rendition of her (as Stephen's) consequences for disturbing the situation. "When the Abbot was wanting for Madeline (as Samuel) to get into his office and I dropped stuff, I guess he felt I shouldn't have been anywhere around there, certainly not dropping things and disturbing the moment. I had no regrets; I knew if needed, I would do it again."

Cyndy said, "How ironic that you ended up getting a penance for helping Samuel when he was getting released from his penance."

Jill added her experience and waved her index finger. "Oh, I know exactly what you mean. When I got back inside from tending to my girls, the hens, I was told to report to the abbot's office. I had no idea what I had done or not done. I felt dizzy as I got closer to his office.

"At first, I was swishing right along, beads clicking. I halted fifteen feet from the hellhole. What have I been doing out of the ordinary today? I didn't even know why I had been led down this rabbit hole. As I was on my knees in front of Abbot Richard, he told me why I was there. Evidently, one of the older brother spies must have tattled on me.

"The abbot said to me, 'It's been reported to me that you were breaking silence while completing your task with the chickens.' When I explained that I was talking enthusiastically to my girls about how well they were doing with their egg production, he reminded me they were not my girls. They were community property that provided food for the community."

She had a look of disgust on her face as she said, "My penance was to kneel holding eggshells from the kitchen."

Caren piped in, "So, did you see me with the heavy wooden box of broken pottery? I was heating some of the pieces that I had thrown on the wheel, and they exploded. It's tricky; you have to slowly raise the temperature in the kiln, and if it gets hot too soon, the pottery will either burst in the kiln or when it is cooling.

"That got reported to the abbot, and I minced my way to his office. My penance was to kneel while holding a few shards of them. I've had some of my pottery burst this century. With no abbot around, there were no penances, just regrets and a mess to pick up. But I have the will to begin again."

There was a chuckle from Mary Jo. "Sorry for laughing, but that was me kneeling next to you holding some broken candles."

If anyone broke anything, they had to kneel for the community of monks to see them holding what they broke. I added my part. "I thought it was a stupid rule. I guess we were supposed to be humiliated or something."

Cordelia (Stephen) laughed. "It just made us giggle silently; it's quite a challenge to giggle with no sound; is it really a giggle? It may have looked like someone was stifling a cough. Fortunately, our robes hid our jiggling bellies. We would undoubtedly receive another penance if we were ever caught giggling and jiggling during such a sacred moment."

It was as if her words opened a sluice that had been blocked with all kinds of detritus. Everyone began nervously laughing, then, giggling so loudly that other people were glancing at them or staring. We did not care. We just wanted to feel good again.

In unison, the members of our group turned in Cyndy's direction, wondering what her story could possibly be.

Without being asked, Cyndy began telling her story, which won the prize for being the scariest: "No one knows, but I had to report that one of the sheep escaped or was stolen; of course, they were my sole responsibility, and you guys helped whenever I asked for help, like with the sheep shearing with those nearly useless excuses for shears.

"To this day, I don't know what happened to Stewy; I still think some scoundrel snuck in and secreted her away. Maybe it was an omen to name her Stewy. Let's have a moment of silence for dear Stewy." Everyone bowed their heads, some stifling a snicker or two.

Cordelia, ever concerned, asked, "But what happened to you?" Your entire insides must have been trembling."

"I tried to pretend to myself and everyone else that nothing had changed. I deceived myself into believing I'd never get found out and that no one would venture outside counting sheep.

"When I was instructing and coordinating the sheep shearing, a senior brother was commissioned to help, ooof. He noticed there was a shortage of wool for our purposes and reported to me that he only counted three sheep, saying he was certain there were originally four."

CHAPTER 44

The Reckoning

THE STOLEN sheep saga continued. With a stressed expression, Cyndy sighed and continued: "I, as John, knew it was no good to lie or deny a missing sheep. It would make matters worse. Lying does seem to have that effect."

Jill was concerned now. "What did you ever do?"

"I knew I was sunk and would soon be summoned to the abbot's office, but I went looking along the perimeter of the fencing to see if I could find any evidence that Stewy could have gotten out on her own; there didn't seem to be any low areas of the stone walls—sheep can jump quite high, however, not as high as those walls."

There were a myriad of possibilities in the group.

Karin speculated, "Could someone have removed some stones and beckoned?" She couldn't help but laugh at the idea of Stewy the sheep wandering the streets.

Mary Jo had another theory: "Cyndy, you mentioned one scoundrel; maybe there wasn't just a single scoundrel; perhaps he had a second scoundrel helping him—could two strong scoundrels lift a sheep the size of Stewy? I'm trying to be serious here, but the name Stewy cracks me up."

Cyndy continued to report on her dilemma. "I finally bit the bullet and headed inside, well aware of the fact that I would soon be on my knees."

Somara tsked as she said, "There's no way to avoid the inevitable reckoning."

Cyndy immediately agreed and said, "Right, so when I told him of my investigations and some of my speculations, which incidentally matched yours, Karin's, and Mary Jo's, he had plenty to say. He did not care if someone stole our sheep; it was vital to our wellbeing.

"He essentially morphed into stolen-sheep-shaming, telling me I'd have to go without woolen mittens, woolen socks, woolen cowls, and possibly a lantern."

I couldn't help but remember how important they were when I had to go out into the bitter cold to milk the cows back in the 16th century. I would have to thank Evelyn (James) once again for the care shown at that time.

"The abbot asked me what we would do if we ran out of wool for the wicks of our lanterns and the entire monastery went into darkness, or if our brothers had to go without socks (referring to the Coptic socks I knitted), with me to thank.

"After haranguing me for what seemed like an eternity, he gave me my penance or sentence: in addition to going without woolen articles, I was to circle the sheep pasture four times a day for a full week, recite the rosary, and pray for the return of the monastery's missing sheep as a reminder that we—he emphasized the next words by yelling them in staccato—HAD FOUR SHEEP."

I gave the air around us time to settle. There was an air of mutual smoldering as several agreed that to make John (Cyndy) go without those vital pieces of woolen clothing during the winter was unjust.

Karin asked, "Which would be worse, having to go without or having to wear double of everything?" drawing on her experience a She said that she was punished by being forced to wear double of everything on a very hot day, and on a free day when we could talk, she kept silent after it was discovered that she talked to one of the brothers from another set, which was a big no-no.

"I remember that day. We were wondering what you were doing wearing a cowl and mittens on such a hot day," said Jill.

Karin retorted with a gallows chuckle and said, "You didn't get to see my double-socked feet in my straining sandals; very uncomfortable."

Mary Jo groaned at that new bit of information. "What a choice. Would you rather suffer from frostbite or heat exhaustion and dehydration?"

Turning the tone to a more positive emphasis, I continued my individual acknowledgments and followed through on my self-promise to thank Evelyn (James): "And sweet Evelyn, you were James, and I know you must have developed your current interest in medicine to become a nurse from way back in the 16th century.

"As James, you helped me when I was such a mess from having to be out in the bitter freeze, milking the cows. It was just a little shed of sorts. I don't know how the poor Jerseys stayed warm with a tiny flame burning for them in a couple of lanterns.

"The tips of my fingers on both hands needed attention, and there you were with your comforting guidance. It's a good thing you had cautioned me to dress warmly, and —

I put on those woolen Coptic socks that you, Cyndy (John), had knitted.

"And thank you, Cyndy (Brother John), for knitting our socks and those warm cowls and mittens, even though it seems Abbot Richard might have thought we'd be throwing rotten tomatoes at you for losing Stewy.

"And you are still knitting today. You even brought some with you. Things were looking pretty bleak for a while at the end. I did think that if and when we ever talked again, I would tease you about our making big money selling the Coptic socks you knitted. I thought they'd be a real crowd-pleaser.

"Sorry to be sticking a knitting needle in the spokes of progress, but I am not going to ever knit those socks in this lifetime," Cyndy said. There was a teasing of moans and 'oh no's' and a raucous round of gallows laughter. Some were patting Cyndy on the back, indicating love and support.

CHAPTER 45

Chapter of Faults

PULLING ON the fresh green grass, I continued to compliment the ladies for their contributions in the 16th century. "Jill, those lovely flowers you, as Francis, grew in your brilliantly colored garden for the chapel, brightened my day."

Cyndy added more. "Even though the chapel was dark and the flickering flame of the lantern brightened things enough, the flowers grown by you and placed just right by Michael (Mary Jo), brightened my spirits, especially when I was so troubled about our dear missing sheep Stewy."

There were voices in unison thanking her and agreeing with the statements.

"Thank you for the help in our Chapter of Faults sessions, where we had to kneel when an offense we were guilty of was announced. What was the point of that anyway?"

Cyndy concluded something valuable: "Maybe in the years before our set landed there, all the penances and acts of humiliation held meaning; maybe it was a holy activity that meant something—to humble them to make them holier, closer to God."

"Right, like asking for food; now that was rough and very difficult to find humor in," Caren agreed. "I think it was mortifying for the person begging for food and the person at the table looking at their brother on his knees, unable to look up at us."

"It was probably just as well that we didn't make eye contact; we may have blown it by getting giggly," thought

Karin countered the image by saying, "I don't know; it seemed some of us were actually caught in the wincing, shameful, embarrassing mindset and posture. Imagine that men who had the opportunity to spoon out whatever they wanted from the serving bowl had to go to another brother, kneel in front of him, and beg for food.

"The kneeling thing was dual effective—it was humiliating for the kneeler and gave the one being kneeled before an icky feeling," she threw her hands up to signal she had said enough, "I could go on, but I will stop here."

Mary Jo admitted Karin was right, saying, "I just wanted to make light of the whole ridiculous and senseless activity."

"I wonder if that's one of the reasons the sets above us could not talk to us, except to say the rosary," Cordelia wondered. They might say something about their secret activity that we could not know about until it was our time."

Inserting my perception about the whole thing, I said, "I remember the mystery and creepiness that hung in the air when we had to stay completely away from the activity room until we were cleared to go near there."

"And then we found out the big secret—it was called the Chapter of Faults," Caren said, echoing my thoughts. "Was it called that because the abbot found fault with us, was exposing our faults, or because we were to admit our faults—or all of the above?" She wondered.

Cordelia chimed in, "That was another thing that made no sense, and because it had no credible purpose, we benefited nothing—nada."

Jill continued venting her original thoughts. "Abbot Richard would say that someone had left their cup on the table rather than returning it to the dishwasher, and that they were to kneel to acknowledge it.

"We all looked around to identify who might have neglected that responsibility; but I'm sure each of us was wondering, as I did, Was it me? Did I forget? Am I right? Is that what you guys were wondering?" She asked.

There were nods of resignation all around.

Jill went on a roll: "Then, when no one acknowledged such an offense, he became more aggressive by threatening that if he didn't see someone kneeling, they would all remain until every recorded offense was acknowledged."

Caren said, continuing Jill's thoughts and observations, "The only solution we had was to just kneel regardless; half of the time, none of us really knew who the guilty one was—should any one of us have acknowledged such an offense?"

Karin had a knack for knowing when and how to make a quick, healing cut. "As long as no one began to believe they had committed the offense, it was okay—I would imagine someone exposed to that environment monthly might actually grow to believe that they had committed the offense they admitted to because of their act of kneeling."

Reluctantly admitting that I have been affected, I said,

"I was making myself a little crazy wondering if I were the only one who should have been on his knees and everyone else could have remained on their bench;

I am heartened how we all hit the floor on our knees when an infraction was announced, so none of us felt alone, and it assuaged the abbot's draconian ways, an allusion to Draco, the 7th century intolerant lawmaker of Athens."

"Oh, Madeline, ever the writer. I am relieved to hear someone say that the Chapter of Faults also impacted them," Cyndy commented, letting out a long sigh.

"Oh, I'm so glad you two are saying that," said Somara.

"Somara, I think you speak for the rest of us." Mary Jo's words were followed by several yeses.

Everyone looked to Karin for a solution, as she gazed toward the white puffy clouds and scratched her head, whispering, "Oh, boy."

CHAPTER 46

A Surprise to All

KARIN, WHO was a psychiatrist, paused for a moment before saying, "Well, I guess we might keep in mind that some may have developed distorted thinking regarding displaced responsibility.

"After the trauma of the 16th century, you may feel unnecessarily responsible for things that are happening around you; that could actually sabotage your day-to-day events and relationships."

I had to step in and say, "Karin, you must have some solution for us who were emotionally wounded."

"This seems just like a good group therapy session, doesn't it?" commented Somara.

There were wide smiles as the others agreed.

"It feels so good, doesn't it?" Mary Jo looked at the others for cohesion.

Cyndy said, "Even though I never found Stewy, I think I will eventually be able to comfort myself knowing he's at the Rainbow Bridge, not being annoyed with sheep shearing or anyone stewing, because he went missing while I was in charge of his well-being for the monastery."

Karin paused while others spoke. Looking to the blue sky, she began. "Okay, here goes. This may sound a bit strange, but every time you hear Abbott Richard's words hovering, picture a little monk on your shoulder whispering lies into your ear, the reasoning part of your brain, and your wounded soul."

Several of the group smiled for the first time in a while. "That just might work," I said as I acted out flicking the medieval whisperer from my shoulder. Everyone followed suit, some saying, "Ping… ping… ping."

It was time to direct praise toward Karin. "The wonderful person who is still helping us must have felt in the dark about many of the incidences referred to in our discussions. That is you, Karin.

"You, as Abraham, were such a blessing for all of us in our set. And you have continued on in the 21st century to help people resolve differences within themselves. Why? We just saw evidence of how effective you are. I felt so badly for you getting thrown out of the monastery.

"I guess I was quite a renegade back then. I'm like Clark Kent, mild-mannered and quiet in this century," I said.

Caren reminded everyone that she was always locked away in the pottery building and missed everything they were talking about. But she did want to find out more, so she asked Karin some questions.

"Karin, I only know a little from what I picked up from the monks' whispers when we were in the monastery. Do you mind if I ask you a few questions?"

"No, certainly not. Ask me anything, and I will fill you in to the best of my ability," replied Karin.

"I've heard there was a dramatic scene circling you. Did you feel like they were going to smother you?"

"O-M-G." This set Karin off. "At first, I felt as if there was no air left to fill my lungs; instead, they were filling up with darkness. When the tribe of importance herded me into the abbot's office, I was frozen with fear.

"I was preparing for some kind of physical beating when I saw the Cardinal with the walking stick," Karin said, with a sigh of relief, remembering that it could have gone harshly but didn't.

Caren continued her questions, "So, they claimed you were an imposter, not even a Catholic?"

Caren had no idea she was slowly gaining information we all felt insecure about. Then, it struck me: It was all literally in the past. We were not throwing around a time-worn idiom. It was real, and we needed to move on. The Karen (Abraham) in front of us was a respectable professional psychiatrist—no phony, no imposter in this lifetime.

Karin explained herself, "Because I only knew what was going on with Abraham while there for the year-long term in the 16th century, I can offer no other information; I actually knew none of Abraham's history, except for the scrambled allegations pronounced by Abbot Richard."

"The assault of accusations was as much a surprise to me as it was to everyone present. What happened to all of us is weird; we were plunked back into a person's body and into a life we lived hundreds of years ago," she added.

Cordelia had been extra quiet during the discussions, but this time she questioned, "Why would our 16th-century persons, or anyone else, ever choose to stay in such a physically, and emotionally confined situation? Did the feeling of being closer to God work for them?"

Mary Jo began the summary by saying, "While immersed in those 16th-century bodies, we had to wing it, in coordination with our assigned person, until we got the hang of it. I think we did well considering the stark circumstances. Let's hope we don't have any long-term psychological effects."

Karin sorted it out as only she could.

CHAPTER 47

Stockholm Syndrome

"I THINK we needed to presume that the life we had dropped into was the way our life would have been in the 16th century. The way the need for survival played out went like this: some were more inclined to believe in the system and the monastic rule, while others acted like they believed. Both group conformed to the rules and behaved accordingly. The answer to all of this is two words: Stockholm Syndrome."

Many exchanged puzzled looks with one another. Cyndy asked everyone's unspoken question, "Is Stockholm Syndrome something related to the bank robbery in Stockholm, Sweden?"

Somara piped up, "Oh yes, I remember now, they said Patty Hearst acted irrationally because of the Stockholm Syndrome."

"But what does that have to do with us?" Mary Jo asked the question that was undoubtedly on everyone's mind.

We leaned in for Karin's wisdom. She said, "The element that creates this syndrome is confusion regarding loyalties. We became endeared to the other monks in our monastery, even Abbot Richard at times.

"We developed a sense of allegiance to them and to the rules. There might even be remnants of loyalty to God thrown in there. The concept of abandoning them became intolerable and morphed into buried efforts, eschewing guilt and breach of trust."

Caren continued Karin's thoughts, saying, "Yuh, because we were stepping into characterizations from centuries ago, we had no context to draw from and had to move through it."

Expressing my same concern,

Evelyn remarked, "I was wondering where I would go if we got evicted; I had no idea about where I had previously resided or where or who my family was."

"We'd all end up with some group of homeless people living somewhere—who knows where; I don't imagine they had homeless shelters back then," Mary Jo said, with a remnant of concern in her voice.

"Do people realize that in our past lives as 16th-century persons, we were really beheaded?" Jill asked abruptly. "I thought we were goners; I'm just glad we, as members of the 21st century, didn't have to re-experience our demise, and the universe spared us," she added.

Cordelia reminded everyone what Jill was referring to. She said that there are two basic ley lines running through the world—just as we have energy waves throughout the atmosphere, so too do we have them within the earth's makeup. The energy below the surface affects the outcomes above.

"The two ley lines that Jill is referring to are called the St. Michael Line and the Mary Line. The Michael Line has a harsh dark feeling to it, while the Mary Line that reaches out around bodies of water has a fluffy energy sensation.

When we travel from one ley line to the area influenced by the other, we sense a noticeable difference," concluded Cordelia.

This opened the door for me to think out loud. "That's how we got into the next lifetimes that led us here—the fluffy Mary energy snatched us away from the dark Michael energy.

"Some of us may have gone together from the 16th century into the next lifetime experience, but others just went alone into a new one to meet individuals we may have known or would know in future lifetimes."

On a roll, I continued, "Shakespeare said something about how we are all actors on a stage; we just keep meeting each other in different parts and roles known as lifetimes,

so we may meet each other in a future lifetime, who knows?"I just hope we are able to detect some similarities that will tie us together."

I often say to people in this lifetime, and they say to me, "We definitely were in some past life together" or "We definitely knew each other in a past life."

Cordelia, who had much knowledge about past lives and had done many readings for people to help them heal from some of their darker times, said, "I have read, been told, or experienced, we will get inklings of what lifetime adventures we may have had. There will be attractions to certain cultures and events, or we may be triggered and repulsed."

"I think feelings and reactions may be especially strong if we believe we were a dark-souled character in some lifetimes. It is difficult for us to forgive our past deeds," she added.

"The thing people need to know is that our soul never changes, regardless of our actions; Buddhists believe the soul is always good," Cyndy said reassuringly.

I thanked Cordelia and Cyndy for clarifying that for us.

Sensing that it was time to move the discussion along, I said, "As I lay prostrate, I couldn't believe when I heard and saw you guys playing harps. Whoa! I felt like I was home, and I didn't feel as isolated anymore."

Somara's eyes lit up as she said, "I was so hopeful hearing them play harps; they were actually playing slightly weird-looking harps, which looked heavy." She squinted inquisitively at the harpists.

Jill probably was full of questions, but she only asked a few: "So how was it playing those clumsy strings of catgut? I can't imagine what those strings must have felt like. I don't know what I'd do with my guitar strung with catgut!"

Several of the harpists laughed, almost with a gallows tone to their laugh.

Caren sighed, lowering her head in a gesture of a heavy burden, and said, "They were heavier than any box of pottery I ever hefted, certainly not streamlined."

Jill's posed another question that I was also perplexed by: "So, how was it you guys knew how to play the harp back in the 16th century?"

CHAPTER 48

The Staircase

CORDELIA CAME through once more, saying that while in the monastery, there was no way of knowing the backstories of our 16th-century characters and what they did as kids, except for those who may have learned the harp in school. She also stated that our experiences in the 16th century must have piqued our interest, leading us to learn what we do today. She made an example of Caren, who is still drawn to pottery-making, and Karin, who works in the field of psychiatry.

Several purring sounds of agreement can be heard as everyone directed their eyes upward to the right, squinching their faces, demonstrating deep consideration, before the tone changed.

The pause gave us the perfect chance to talk about the eternal stairs. "Do we want to attempt those steps?" I asked, pointing to the staircase, which was missing a handrail. I told them that it has "religious pilgrimage" written all over it, where people pray on every step—that would be a lot of praying. "There had to be an easier way," I added.

There were several moans. "I might just sit this one out," stated Mary Jo.

Random yeses can be heard in agreement, and then Cyndy suggests the labyrinth. "Remember, we were going to play our harps as we walked the labyrinth?"

I couldn't help but be a bit sour with my reply, saying, "Yuh, walking up the trail that they used to drag the Abbott and his assistants to their death, sounds like a cheerful activity."

"But," Jill pointed out, "labyrinths are very healing, so maybe we should take that path."

"So, are you saying we should take the labyrinth path to the top?" Somara spoke as she weighed the possibilities and the pros and cons.

"Yuh, if we can get there. It was just a thought." said, adding that since it has been five centuries since it was used to transport the monks to the gallows, it is uncertain whether the path still exists.

Somara enlightened the others by sharing that there is so much written about this place and that she never thought that what she had read , someday, come in handy. She said that the ancients carved the spiral terraces to make it easier to journey up to the top and to carry or drag with them needed items like stones.

Interrupting Somara, Mary Jo remarked sarcastically, "Yuh, it was easier to carry bodies to the top—I have a feeling our leaders from the monastery weren't the only ones who died on this earthen mound."

Somara went on to say that there are numerous theories as to why there was such an unusual terracing around this giant hill.

"Yet, the path is patterned like a labyrinth, so why or who used it?" sked.

"This place is old." Mary Jo concluded, confirming what several of us had been struggling to comprehend.

I admitted to the others that I still can't grasp how old other countries are in comparison to the United States.

Evelyn agreed with me, saying that we've become lost in our own little world, that we've become blind to the incredible realities of ancient tales, and that we've spent our energies smoldering about our country's short history with its intolerable conflicts.

"I see where you're going with this," said, ing. "We are just a fresh dab of paint on a giant canvas of ancient accumulations of brush strokes,

like a wet clay pot beside ancient collections filling shelves in museums of ancient history," she said, looking around the group for other comparisons.

Jill raised her hand for emphasis when she said, "It's like putting a young sapling beside a chunk of petrified wood."

Cordelia laughed at a thought she couldn't help but share. "I think we're going way back to the bobby socks of the 1950s."

I chuckled and said, "Ooof, that was a long time ago."

Cordelia continued, "Let's put those old ankle-cuffed socks beside…"

"Don't you say it…" interjected jokingly.

"Let's put those old ankle-cuffed socks right next to the good ole Coptic socks."

Cyndy knew that things were getting out of hand, so she said that there was no way she'd knit those freakishly-shaped socks so we could all have a pair to wear with our sandals.

"I already told Madeline that we're not going to market those monstrosities in this century, and besides, it's time for us to look for a way up to the top of this ominous hill," she added.

Karin came to Cyndy's aid, saying, "She's right; I don't think we can comfortably approach the path from here." Karin stood up and kicked the overgrown weeds and crabgrass around, attempting to find signs of a medieval path. "I think we're too far down to start walking the more groomed labyrinth," she explained.

"Does anyone have any guides to get up there?" I laughed at my question. "Ooof, we might have snatched one when we passed through the portal."

Cordelia, knowing she could get away with teasing me, replied, "Ah, bummer, I must have left mine in the giant pocket of my monk's habit."

Mary Jo, on the other hand, was the one who came up with the best suggestion to solve our dilemma. She suggested that perhaps we could find someone around here who could tell us if there was another way up to the top besides those treacherous steps.

CHAPTER 49

Communication
Problems

WE ALL thought that Mary Jo was the clearest thinker and most knowledgeable about how to get to the top of the tor. I hoped for a helicopter to come to our rescue, as I had previously fantasized in similar situations. It could easily lift us up there in about a minute.

It looked like we'd make this long journey up the stone staircase by the end of the day. The ascent would be bad enough, but without a rail, I worry that we might pitch forward on the way down.

As always, no large-capacity helicopter, nor a small one, was coming for us. I told myself that I needed to get a grip and focus.

When I could finally think logically, I said, "Let's do what Mary Jo has suggested." I told everyone to fan out, find us a way up there, and then come back here to compare notes.

I decided to approach a group but quickly lost courage after overhearing their conversation. The taller woman said, "Musimy wejść po długich schodach."

Her friend laughed and replied, "Cieszę się, że zjadłem dobre śniadanie."

My first thought was to run the other way, but since we were on a mission, I went up to them, bit the bullet, and outrightly asked, "Is there another way up besides the stairs?" I gestured going up the steps and walking on a level path while pointing to the stairs.

Needless to say, they looked at me strangely. They probably thought I was a mime looking for money, expecting me to hold up a money-collection cup.

They all shrugged and said, "Bez angielskiego, no English."

I nodded and said, "Gracias." Ooof, that went well. Not!

The next group spoke in English. They did, however, ask me the same question about a safer way to climb the stairs.

I was feeling increasingly deflated. I just hoped the others had better luck. I moped my way back to the meeting spot, where I found some people already seated on the grass beneath the tree.

Their grumbling gave me no hope.

As I neared the group, Jill looked up at me and asked, "Doesn't anyone speak English here? We're in England for Gods' sakes."

Karin shook her head, explaining that those who spoke English were in the same boat as us—looking for a safer way up the tor; if one even existed.

This reminded me of the nightmare I had during my trip to Mexico, so I shared my experience with language barriers to the group.

I went to Mexico with a friend a few years ago. When we arrived at our resort, I made the mistaken assumption—which really means that I would embarrass you and me—that everyone at the Holiday Inn spoke English. Apparently, the resort's employees don't learn different languages in order to kowtow to their guests.

One fellow was quite remarkable in that he spoke Mayan at his home, Spanish at his workplace, and fluent English as well for tourists like of us. Another guy was amusing; he'd greet me with "Ola," and I'd respond with "O-law," and he'd joke with me, "O-luh, o-luh, Coco-Cola."Another nightmare was discovering that no one spoke English at the airport. It was difficult to find out when our flight's boarding time was. We only saw a screen that flashed "delayed," and that was it. We had no idea whether we were supposed to be boarding the same plane when we saw camera footage of passengers boarding because no one spoke English. This caused us a lot of stress. After an hour, we heard an announcement telling us to go downstairs to board our plane. As we went down, we met an English-speaking woman who informed us that she had been waiting for two hours and that the flight had been delayed the entire time.

After I finished rambling, Cyndy said something humorous. "With so many different nationalities and languages, could that be like the Tower of Babel?" she asked, pointing to the looming tower at the top.

Evelyn suggested that because we know so little about the tor and its surrounding areas, Cyndy might be correct.

Mary Jo, being the most knowledgeable member of the group, shared what she remembered from what she'd read. She claimed that the tor was once a cathedral steeple and that there was a St. Michael Church and several buildings in the area, but that they were all destroyed at some point, leaving only the steeple.

I could feel my bitterness returning. "I wonder if that was before or after the gallows were constructed for the leaders of ou—the monastery; I almost said our monastery," I exclaimed, flustered.

Jill reminded us that we were there in the past, so that was our monastery. Despite how horrible many aspects of it were, it was a home where we were sheltered and fed. Jill added that we were the reason Abbot Richard did not want to close the monastery because he felt responsible for us.

"With no backstory of who we'd been before the monastery, we'd definitely have nowhere to go," said Evelyn.

Somara summed it up, saying, "I guess we should thank the abbot, whoever and wherever he is today."

The inner dowser, Cordelia, became reflective. "I feel like our solution might be on the left side of this massive hill, so maybe we should take that route," she suggested.

The thought of standing up brought back an old, familiar feeling—hesitation. I observed that everyone was moving their bodies in various ways and shuddering as if they were shaking off painful memories of their medieval nightmares.

In preparation for the trek, a few of us searched the ground for a walking stick. "If we ever find ourselves walking on a steep path going up, we will be grateful that we took the time to choose a suitable stick," reassured

CHAPTER 50

Visions of People

EVERYONE LOOKED around and found a decent, sturdy walking stick. They held on to their walking sticks as a symbol of hope. Additionally, Cordelia suggested that we envision ourselves finding a path devoid of stairs. She also encouraged all of us to call for it because she strongly feels that it exists.

We could practically hear each other chanting to the universe, asking for the path to appear, as we followed Cordelia's advice. With each call, our hope was beginning to dwindle, and our faith in Cordelia's inner dowsing abilities was wearing thin.

Suddenly, Karin announced that she could see tiny specks of people high up on the hill. As we stopped to take it all in, Caren remarked that the people were moving downward, so there must be a second path besides those stairs at the front.

Our hopes may have been restored at that point, but Evelyn sighed at the thought of the ascent up the dirt or concrete path and said, "I sure hope there aren't any stairs to climb in that tower."

Evelyn and anyone else who was concerned were relieved by Mary Jo's explanation that the steeple was hollow and that it was the only structure still standing after the St. Michael church had been destroyed around the time that Abbot Richard and the other two monks (Roger and John) were executed.   The stairs at the front, which are inclined at a 45-degree angle, lack railings. This prompted Cyndy to open a discussion about it in order to hopefully divert everyone's attention away from the overwhelming sense of futility.

Mary Jo brought up the possibility that there wasn't enough metal rail; after all, it is over 400 feet high. The upkeep of the metal rails, in

Somara's opinion, might be too much. Jill, on the other hand, believes that installing railings would only serve to attract destructive gangs of people, which are present anywhere in the world. The conclusion of the discussion was that everyone understood why there were no railings. Although everyone had different perspectives on the issue, I was glad and thankful to Cyndy for opening up the discussion.

Caren, who had been fastidiously watching for motion on the hill, reported what she'd observed. "I still hope that we can get up to the top of the hill without having to find ourselves staring down on those formidable stairs," she said, echoing my sentiment.

I noticed and told the group that there now appeared to be people halfway up the hill, moving in our direction. They seem to be suspended in midair.

Cordelia, with her hand covering her eyes from the sun, stared in that direction and commented, "I wonder if they are walking around the labyrinth?"

"So have we been betting on the wrong group that is descending?" I whimpered.

Karin pointed to a group coming toward us on our level on the ground and said, "There's got to be someone who speaks either English or one of the few languages we can clumsily decipher." She blew a raspberry to conclude her statement.

Cordelia and I glanced in the direction Karin had indicated. We looked knowingly at one another, certain that we were thinking the same thing.

Cordelia approached me and eagerly shared her inner dowsing intuition with me first. She asked, "Do you notice anything different in their aura?"

Madeline had the ability to pick up energy from others. Some people saw auras in specific colors. There're books written instructing their readers that certain colors indicated information about various levels, physical, emotional, psychological, and spiritual.

Madeline never went by those books. Her core reference and its meaning were derived from her own experience observing energy colors surrounding a person and what was going on with them. It had nothing to do with electrical or magnetic energy.

She remembered having this ability confirmed when she read 'Celestine Prophesy' by James Redfield. What a compelling book. It changed yet another aspect of her life. Madeline was thrilled to know there was an online reading of this book on YouTube.

This way others might understand they have the ability to see auras of plants, animals, objects, and people. The 3rd chapter explains how if we lightly squint at any of these, we will see a shadow just above them.

Some people see a color on a deeper level, and they might be able to make a chart in their mind of how they feel about these different colors.

Madeline knew what she was seeing with the people coming toward her and the meaning of the glowing brilliant white light surrounding them.

CHAPTER 51

· · · · · · · · · · · · · · · ·

We Know Who You were

CORDELIA RESPONDED to her own question. "Their aura travels out exceptionally far and is pure white. I would never expect to find anyone with a clear and balanced aura with the dark and negative Mickhael ley line crossing here."

Feeling less alone in my vision. "Hopefully, we can investigate the cause. Cool, they are getting closer. Hello."

English responses were all we heard, thankfully.

"Hey," said the girl wearing a lovely hat of various colored butterflies. Although I made an effort not to be rude, I couldn't help but stare because I recognized a few of the butterflies.

But I thought that if you wear a hat that looks like a poster, expect to be stared at or studied.

"Hi," said the sportily dressed one, who had a baseball cap with the letters NY. The lady in the flamboyant sun hat said hello too.

We returned the greetings. Next came our barrage of questions.

Cordelia began. "So, are you guys coming down from the top?"

The butterfly lady responded, "Yes, we finally made it back down. We went up those treacherous steps in front of this monstrosity of a hill but Gloria," pointing to the sporty one, "discovered there was a stairless backway up or down."

Gloria stepped closer to explain how she spotted the cement path heading downward. "Hi, yes, I knew anything would be better than that dizzying, steep, and railless stairway, plunging downward."

Butterfly lady introduced herself and her other companion. "Excuse my rudeness; my name is Mary and this is Anne." She gestured with her arm extended.

Anne stepped forward and began shaking hands with everyone. "It is so good to meet you and possibly be able to share our bizarre experience."

In my jumbled head, I quickly made mental notes. Butterfly hat was Mary, sports cap was Gloria, and sun hat was Anne. I forewent the order of introducing ourselves in the order of age. Instead, I introduced myself, quickly went through the roll call, and left it to everyone to make acquaintances. And they did. It was fun to see the enthusiasm until the tone grew more serious.

Mary began the harsh declaration. "We are worn out. We do not understand what has happened to us since we got here.

"One of the most bizarre occurrences was on our first drive up this way. We did not know we were supposed to get a shuttle ride up here.

"We impulsively headed up toward the signs for the Tor. Our trip up the hill through downtown was worse than the ride back down.

"I don't think we even reexamined the distorted faces as we descended the hill, supporting the shops full of busy, preoccupied individuals."

Gloria agreed with the report. "We three had similar reactions to the townsfolk. I heard inner screaming, and Anne saw a sick green color around them."

Anne said, "There was an olive-green fog around the whole town."

Mary compared her account of the events to a more current physical symptom as she spoke for the trio. "The strangest, most unnerving thing that happened was that our throats felt tighter the closer we got to the top of this Tor."

Anne added her description while holding on to her throat to simulate that life-threatening sensation. "It was as if something or someone were clenching my throat right by my air pipe." After taking a deep breath, she continued, "I began panicking when I experienced difficulty breathing."

Gloria claimed that she started coughing and put her hands to her throat, saying, "I didn't know if I was allergic to something or if the climb up had affected my breathing. I began wheezing as if there wasn't enough oxygen."

Mary summarized by saying, "We figured maybe the altitude was too much for us. Next, the most debilitating thing happened. I had just reached the top of the staircase, and I was hit with a case of vertigo like I've never had before."

When Anne asked Mary if she'd ever had vertigo, Mary answered, "No."

Gloria was showing concern for us. "So, we don't want to say too much and influence your trek up the path, but I will tell you that the path we came down seems a lot easier than those death-defying steps we climbed.

"I will give you a heads-up, though. The 45-degree angle hill is quite short, although the section where the path levels off is extremely long," Gloria added.

Mary said, "Yuh, hopefully, this place doesn't affect you the way it did us."

Gloria added an important detail. "As we examined each other, a discoloration that totally encircled each of our necks began to show."

"Gloria, let's not forget about your black eyes and swollen lips that creepily appeared," Anne said shuddering.

The worst, according to Mary, was the excruciating physical pain they felt as they neared a plaque marking a certain monk's grave. "I think his name was Richard," she said.

"I felt like my arms were being yanked out of their sockets. Fortunately, they have benches up there. I had to sit; my legs would no longer support me. I felt paralyzed. Gloria's face and jaw ached like a toothache, and she had humming in her ears, making her feel nauseous and crazy," Mary added.

"I had shooting pain from my tailbone to the top of my neck," said Anne, drawing a line in the air with her finger to accentuate the extent of the area of pain.

All three looked at us and simultaneously and us asked the same question. "What would cause such a thing?"

Our group listened intently to what the three ladies were saying, and as we did, it became clear to us who these three women were in the 16th century.

But how to tell them was going to be the challenge.

CHAPTER 52

Slow the Cadence

I HAD been doing some quick thinking about how to continue the conversation with the new insight provided to us. To use a time-worn idiom, "This changes everything."

We had some major work to do with these ladies, our former leaders from the 16th century. Yes, they were our former leaders, and here we are requesting further leadership as to how to get up that blasted hill.

The irony is that when we saw them being dragged out through our monastery door, we never dreamed we would meet them again, alive, in a new lifetime—ours. Another irony is that we, the subordinates, would be leading them in their healing. I puzzled over where start and how to do it.

Since it would be seriously impolite to call a huddle with the other ladies, I was on my own. I could only hope they joined in with some affirmations for me.

I decided to just go for it, starting from the beginning. In the words of Julie Andrews as Maria from The Sound of Music, "a very good place to start."

"Did any of you notice any unusual sensations before getting to Glastonbury? The reason I ask is because Cordelia began experiencing extreme discomfort on our way to and when we were within the vision of the Tor."

I looked at my companions and said, "I don't know if either Cordelia or I have mentioned this to any of you, but you will soon see how it makes complete sense."

Turning my attention to Mary, Gloria, and Anne, I continued, "We both complained of severe headaches. As we drove closer to the Tor, our head pain increased, in addition to a new sensation."

Mary Jo, Somara, Evelyn, Cyndy, Karin, and Caren looked from one to the other. I guess we hadn't told anyone about the strange foreshadowing. The three women were fixated on my every word.

Cordelia jumped in to help me out. "Our headaches morphed into a very weighted feeling, like our heads were being held down. Now we know why."

Mary Jo wanted to make some sense of things for the bewildered trio. "We've actually just come out of a time warp where we were all monks in the monastery during the 16th century in Glastonbury."

Cyndy added her take on things. "Evidently, that did happened to all of us, which is why we've been called by the universe to meet beforehand—at a workshop about harps—which we will explain further if desired."

Somara gifted us with knowledge she gained from being the bursar, or money manager, for the monastery. "Because the monastery was making money fast, the King during that time, Henry VII, demanded to shut down the monasteries in England.

Our leader, Abbot Richard Whiting, didn't want us, his monks, his charges, to be displaced. Because he refused, there was nothing but trouble from then on."

To make Mary, Gloria, and Anne understand the impact of what happened, she said, "To begin with, the King's henchmen forced their way in through a locked and barricaded door."

Karin admitted she wasn't there but reported what she'd heard. "I'm choosing to relate this to you, because as a psychiatrist, I am aware of the subtle workings of the mind." In an effort to be cautious and gentle, she slowed her cadence as she continued, "You may have unforeseen reactions upon hearing the next set of events these others have witnessed.

What you have already experienced as you were nearing the top of the Tor will hopefully all make sense and will impact you as needed."

Karin took a deep breath before she pronounced what might potentially cause new trauma for Anne, Gloria, and particularly, Mary. "When the King's soldiers violently entered the monastery, they made a death announcement for our three leaders—

Richard Whiting, Roger James, and John Thorne. They were to be brought to the Tor to be hanged to death. Although, Richard would be cut down sooner to be kept alive for the sake of torturing."

All three began to hold onto their throats, with the rope marks returning. It was uncanny how quickly those marks appeared on each of their throats. There were moans and puzzled facial expressions.

Mary was the first to be able to put emotions and questions into coherent words. "What do you mean by all of this? Are you saying we were all in a monastery in the 16th century? How could this be? Do you people believe in past lives?"

CHAPTER 53

••••••••••••••••••

Healing Takes Place

CAREN LOOKED around at the others leading the gallows guffaw. "Well, if any of us did not know about or believe in past lives, we definitely do now."

Somara, the fact-finder, presented helpful information. "I can give some theological background to what may have happened to us. There is a sect of Judaism and another one called Druzism that asks if after we die we come back in another body in a different period of time. It is clear that at one time we had male equipment and at some point, some era, some lifetime, we came back with female equipment."

Somara continued to elaborate. "Druzism believes that when we die, our souls enter the body of a newborn. They believe that the soul needs to be connected with a body. That doctrine is called traducianism."

Karin, speaking from personal investigation, had some eye-opening information as well. "Many Jews are surprised to learn that reincarnation—the idea that souls revolve through numerous lifetimes—is a basic principle of Judaism."

Gloria posed the next question. "So, you're proposing the possibility that we all knew each other in another lifetime, and maybe that's part of why we just encountered each other, to help further sort it out?"

Anne wanted more clarification. "Do you think the fact we had such violent physical reactions is evidence that we indeed were Richard Whiting, Roger James, and John Thorne?"

Mary said," We can play a game of Who was Who in the 16th century."

Gloria decided to participate. "Well, since I developed blackening around my eyes and a sudden aching in my jaw, I will wager that I was Brother James in that past life."

There were nods of agreement and various verbal responses.

"Right."

"It looks like it."

"Sad to say, it sounds so."

Cordelia asked, "How are you doing about it?"

Karin spoke up and sparked the healing when she asked, "Gloria, does this help any?"

Just as Gloria was about to respond, Anne pointed at Gloria's eyes. "Gloria, your eyes are back to normal; even the bloodshot effect is gone."

Gloria was hopeful. "What does my neck look like?"

Gloria's neck appeared to be in good condition, and Anne smiled as she said, "That looks normal too. What about mine, any rope marks on it?"

Gloria had a big grin when she hugged Anne. "No, no markings either."

Mary was incredulous, watching her two friends heal right before her eyes. "Mn't hurting anymore, so what about my neck? How does that look?"

"Look, I can do a little dance, probably not the Irish or Scottish dance, but I couldn't do that kind of dancing before," Mary said.

Both Gloria and Anne approached Mary to inspect her throat area. Everyone clapped when they found no marks.

Evelyn gave them her best wishes, saying, "Hopefully, this is enough for your healing, and you won't have to take the time trip, as we seemed to have done."

Cordelia was still curious about their bright auras. She asked, "So, did you guys go any place or visit any particular spots when you got to the top? You obviously picked up some major positive energy somewhere."

Cordelia continued to explain. "The energy you were emanating as you were coming closer to us indicated to Madeline and me that you'd already healed some or had balanced the negative and the positive energy."

Remembering what Cyndy had said earlier, that walking the labyrinth is healing, Cordelia asked, "Did you, by any chance, walk any of the labyrinth up there?"

"Yes, we did walk that ancient path," Anne answered with pride.

Cyndy reminded everyone that they had considered playing their harps in the labyrinth. "I think we will feel renewed if we walk a section of the labyrinth," she shared.

Gloria shared some information they'd received but didn't quite understand. "We were told about the energy channels called ley lines, whatever those are."

Mary helped Gloria out, saying, "Yuh, they said that two of these ley lines called St. Michael and Mary are quite opposite. The Michael line is harsh and has dark negative energies, whereas the Mary line is sweet, full of light, and positive."

Anne remembered an important fact: if those two lines cross, healing and balance can take place. "We were instructed to stand in the middle of the steeple."

Gloria enthusiastically reported that you could actually see where people had stood there. "There were shoe print indentations in the cement floor. It was amazing."

Cordelia resumed her questioning. "So, each of you stood within the walls of the steeple? That's amazing. So, the two opposing ley lines cross right at the top? Whoa! I want to go up there as soon as possible."

CHAPTER 54

The Summit

I WANTED to wrap up things so we could get moving, so I asked, "Is there anything else we should know?"

The three looked at each other, shrugged, and shook their heads in a no gesture.

I was sensing a piece of sadness as we prepared to say adieu. We'd probably never see each other again in this lifetime anyway. But possibly and most probably, in another, we will.

Evelyn, our concerned nurse with knowledge beyond ours, came forward. "Hold up a minute. We've been standing here for a while, so our hearts have had time to quiet.

It is a perfect opportunity to check your heart rates. Some of you may already be aware of yours. Do you know how to check your resting heart rate? We are going to be exerting some serious stress on our hearts as we climb that hill.

If you feel your heart pounding out of your chest, just stop and give it a rest. Make sure you let your walking stick do most of the work. I'll remind everyone to check their heart rate partway up."

Everyone began discussing what their typical resting rate was or is. Cyndy, Somara, and I all had 60 beats per minute because we regularly engage in physical activity.

Somara walks up and down hills and rides a bicycle. Cyndy walks for an hour three times a week at work and jogs on her days off. I used to jog; however, now I am more apt to slog or slow jog.

We readied our walking sticks as I pointed my chin toward the nearing entrance to the walking path.

We couldn't see the top because the initial incline was at an angle of about 45 degrees. We blindly chugged toward the top. The payoff was that it soon leveled out. This was the point at which Evelyn noted that everyone should check their pulse rate.

The knowledgeable nurse said, "If you have doubled your resting rate, you've performed some excellent aerobic work. The next looks like a long haul as it levels out, but it will give our hearts some relief as it will require no climbing exertion."

After we climbed yet another 45-degree-angled hill, the tower, which had been hidden by the hills, gradually revealed its entire form. Though it involved less walking than the previous one, we were out of breath.

Standing at the top, we felt like Rocky Balboa, but sadly, no brass was playing for us.

Still, out of breath, Cyndy cheered, "We're finally up here. Now we can check out the labyrinth."

Catching her breath, Cordelia remarked, "Speaking of the labyrinth, I'm so glad we decided not to schlep our harps all the way up here; it was difficult enough to drag myself up here."

Observant Caren noticed two vacant benches. Pointing her two index fingers in the direction of the empty seats, she said, "We'd better make a beeline for those benches."

We quickly headed toward them. Evelyn opened her mouth widely, quietly yelling in slow motion, "Noooooo."

We were too late. The empty spots were now occupied. We need to look for another one.

As I looked around, I realized we ascended opposite the stairs. It would have been more reassuring if we'd known this ahead of time, but we wouldn't know this unless we were up here.

Guess where Cyndy saw one? You guessed it, down a short path and a bit beyond, to the labyrinth. It looked like we were going to be walking some length of the labyrinth regardless.

Feeling more rested, Mary Jo said, "It's coming back to me now; this labyrinth was used for ceremonies."

Cordelia bitterly asked a good question: "Before or after the lynching of our leaders and newly-met friends—Mary, Anne, and Gloria?"

Mary Jo shrugged sadly as she answered Cordelia's question. "Probably during and even long before."

Caren, the artist and potter, said in a dreamy tone, "Picture it— lights from lanterns and candles, songs and dancing."

Somara sang the next auditory image while waving her arms. "Then, we hear flutes and harps and dancing virgins twirling in lovely artistic patterns."

After we had rested, we were actually pumped to walk a portion of the labyrinth and maybe even dance some of it.

· · · · · · · · · · · · · · · · · ·

CHAPTER 55

The End of the Story

AS WE rose in ceremony from our resting benches, I was compelled to ask a strange question: "Does anyone else hear low-volume flutes, or is it my tinnitus? I know I often have varied tones of buzzing in my ears, but this sounds different."

Mary Jo, Caren, and Somara simultaneously responded, saying, "I thought it was my tinnitus. Yuh, I thought the altitude was affecting my tinnitus, and I thought my stress was agitating mine."

Evelyn said, "It is faint, but I don't think it's your tinnitus. Let's wait to see if it gets any louder."

"Good idea. Then it may become clearer," Cyndy and Karin said, agreeing with Evelyn.

Cyndy suggested we continue walking along the nicely manicured section of the labyrinth.

Caren did a few twirls as the subtle sounds became louder. Cyndy, who was in her glory, joined in, finally being able to set her dancing feet on the labyrinth path.

Mary Jo stopped, tilted her head, bent lower, and said, "Are my eyes deceiving me? There appear to be lights floating below us. No, wait a minute, now they are changing directions, swerving in columns hither and yon like a river." Her voice became higher in pitch as she progressed in her announcement.

Cordelia experienced the same vision as Mary Jo and was enthused about it. "Oh, I see them now; they appear to be ascending through deep tangled grass in areas showing less attention to upkeep, such as here."

"They look like a lovely swarm of lightning bugs that I might see outside my home on a summer's eve," Somara waxed poetically. She could have chosen a more ethereal metaphor for swarm, but it was off the cuff.

Then we heard loud, explosive sounds echoing off the Tor and throughout the valley. However, they did seem to be following a pattern and rhythm.

The flutes grew louder. Had we walked through another portal, returning to the 16th century? It was clearly Renaissance music played on Renaissance musical instruments. I dared not mention it to the others. They were probably in their own nightmare of wonder.

Our anxiety grew as we stood there. Cyndy suggested we return to our benches to see what was to ensue. We all agreed and followed her lead. Not much more dancing took place within our hearts or on our feet.

We sat there motionless for what seemed like hours, fixated on the lights approaching from the base of the long hill.

Hearing the harps made us wonder if it had anything to do with the fact that we'd all been beheaded in the 16th century. In movies, there has always been harp music played after someone dies.

Evelyn was the first one to speak. "This is more than eerie; if we didn't have the same benches we sat on earlier, I'd think that we had gone back to the 16th century."

Evelyn had thrown open the sluice gate. She expressed everyone's fear and/or terror. There were several mewls.

Cordelia expressed her greatest dread. "I do not want to relive a single minute of the 16th century."

"Or any aspect of medieval times; not one second of it," Karin added.

Then I recalled the horrible events in Karin's life as she lived through hell. She was the 16th-century Brother Abraham, who helped everyone but was eventually expelled in shame and condemnation.

Cyndy was worried that she'd once again be scorned for losing her precious sheep, whom she affectionately named Stewy. "She was my responsibility, and Abbot Richard never let me forget it."

In an effort to comfort Cyndy, Karin reminded her of who we had recently discovered the Abbot to be in this lifetime. "I'm sure if you talked to Mary, formerly Abbot Richard, she would absolve you of any wrongdoings."

"I don't think I could create any more 16th-century pottery after the luxury of the pottery-making techniques I've become accustomed to this century," confessed Caren.

Mary Jo, another confessant, spoke up. "I'd also never want to go back and spend my days attempting to see anything in the clouded darkness of that chapel. It's a wonder I didn't lose my eyesight, though I could never determine my degree of visual acuity because I never had to. I was like a mole, unlike most of you who got to be out in the fresh air."

"Any light and fresh air I happened to steal was a teaser," Somara begrudgingly reminded us. "Answering the door and accepting money for the next order of penance to be undertaken for the donor's intentions afforded me my snatch of daylight and pure oxygen."

"I miss my harp soooo much," Cordelia moaned, "those catgut harps could hardly be called harps; I don't ever want to see one, even in a museum, and I may have developed an aversion to wet wood, like you, Madeline. Bwaaa."

As the smoldering air around us died away, I became aware of another sound. "Bells! Does anyone else hear bells, or has my tinnitus gone into overdrive?"

Evelyn said reassuringly, "No, those are clearly bells you are hearing."

"I see heads beginning to appear," Cyndy said, pointing to the direction where chanting, flutes, drums, harps, and bells on some kind of rack can be heard.

We were wary as one of the dancing maidens motioned for us to join them. The whole thing was too bizarre. We looked at each other, shrugged, and rose from our self-established safe space.

The scene is reminiscent of a page torn from a book containing Escher paintings. We accepted their invitation to join them and become a part of the optical illusion.

As they marched, with us in tow, it occurred to me, as a friend once said, "What goes down must come up." The procession was heading back down the hill they'd come up.

I wanted to start communicating through cupped ears. "If we kept following this procession, we'd have to walk all the way back up, which we've already done today."

The first to hear me was Cyndy. "I'll pass it along," she said. "I hope it doesn't end up getting messed up like in the game Telephone."

I hoped that was everyone's wish that we head back up to the steeple. I know that Cordelia was very interested when Gloria, one of the women who descended from the Tor, mentioned that the floor within the steeple had foot indentations and was where the two opposing Michael and Mary ley lines crossed.

I knew our project was a success when I saw our group gradually pull back and turn around.I got on my proverbial soapbox as I

stood at the entrance to the steeple's passageway. From beginning to bitter end, this entire experience has led me to reflect on Enlightenment. The concept is sometimes accompanied by the phrases "Chop wood, carry water before enlightenment; chop wood, carry water after enlightenment.

We don't change our tasks from lifetime to lifetime to lighten our burden; we change our perceptions. One fact is clear to me: things will continue to get easier.

The Inquisition and other such horrors would no longer be tolerated. As we progress from one new lifetime to the next, our lives will change, and we will improve and grow closer to enlightenment.

Hopefully, we will recognize some aspects of each other over the course of our various lifetimes. I suggest that we each do what the Native Americans have done for at least 14,000 years: strengthen and bring the spiral of our lives into balance.

I am heading over to where the harsh, dark Michael line crosses with the fluffy, light-filled Mary line. With my feet firmly planted, I will bring the harshness I have experienced in previous and current lifetimes into light and balance.

As I scanned the panorama of greens of hope and browns of conviction, I knew for certain that my life was in balance and that I'd be okay.

THE END OF THE STORY (In this Lifetime)